My
Name Was
Susan O'Malley

a novel

Michael J. Nercessian

ISBN (paperback): 979-8-9854659-0-7
ISBN (ebook): 979-8-9854659-1-4

For Jodi —
Thank you for laughing at all my jokes
though I'm seldom funny.

1

My name was Susan O'Malley.
You probably don't remember me.

2

Mags doesn't know I drink. Not the social turning of the wrist, a whiskey served neat with colleagues after hours or pints with my childhood friends at the local. Of those, she's keenly aware and even, on occasion, encourages. It's the others, on the nights when sleep eludes me—most nights—when the curling finger coaxes me into the snare. The little drinks, three fingers of warm gin after Mags heads off to bed to count sheep or the rum straight from the bottle on a weekend morning before the day's chores—those are the troubling ones. But that's all in the past.

The house is quiet these days save the settling of the floorboards and occasional drone of voices leaking from the unwatched television. Our daughter, Lily, married and moved out, and Margaret and I have little left to say. It's not an uncomfortable quiet, just quiet. The house itself is too large for the two of us and in need of a growing family to fill it, to give it purpose again. I don't like being alone with my thoughts.

I'm sitting on the front porch on a lazy Sunday morning watching the world. The ceiling of the porch is water-stained, yellow and brown, and needs repair, and the white support columns beg for a fresh coat of paint. The morning air is thick and warm and smells like an approaching thunderstorm. Summer in Massachusetts. My coffee has gone cold. I thought I wanted it, but it sat untouched as my mind wandered. I attempt to stretch my back, twisting, turning in the seat. My spine no longer cracks like a young man's, but rather shifts into a new position with a hellish scrape like two ocean-polished rocks being rubbed together. What was I thinking about? No one. Nothing. Everything.

"Good morning."

There's a man on my front porch.

"Good morning," I reply with little attempt to hide my irritation. "Can I help you?"

He's dressed well enough: blue-collared button down shirt and khaki pants, brown English shoes. His hair, mostly reddish-brown with flecks of grey, was recently cut tight with care. His hands are empty, no supplies ready for quick distribution, no pamphlets espousing the benefits of alternate interpretations of ancient books, nothing that would cause suspicion except whatever he's carrying under his arm.

"This is 1750 Crescent Street, correct?"

"Yes."

"Are you Tom Burns?"

"I'm sorry, who are you?"

It's easy to say now that he was somehow familiar, the air about him, the way he stood, very straight, confident, like he owned the room. I didn't want to like him immediately, but I did.

"I'm Patrick O'Malley," he says and smiles. "Susan's brother."

Margaret is standing behind the screen door, watching us from the shadows, two ghosts shaking hands.

"This is Susan's brother," I say.

"Patrick," he offers and bows his head like he'd been sent to finishing school.

"Yes," she says through the screen. "I heard."

Yes, it's him, matinee idol handsome, yet still a boyish grin—I'd last seen him at Susan's funeral, nine, maybe ten years old, his face pale, stoic against the day, unable to comprehend his older sister had met such an end. And after forty years, on a late June lazy Sunday morning at 10am, the curse has arrived on our doorstep.

Such a plain, ordinary name, "Patrick", yet he makes things… complicated. He brings old family photographs stuffed into a shoebox he carries under his arm like a football and places it in the center of the coffee table then sighs, like he's returned something we didn't know we'd lost. Margaret and I look at each other out of the corners of our eyes.

"I found these in my parent's attic after my mother passed. They're mostly of Susan, of course," he says in a windy, rehearsed voice before lifting the lid of the box with a magician's flair. The only thing missing from the performance is a half-hearted "ta-da!" and a spindly white rabbit pulled from the box by his ears.

Susan. I haven't thought of her since our time at Stevens College—since those four lawless years of purgatory before adult life begins. These were supposed to be the best years of our lives, a time to fall in love, question ancient philosophers and protest foreign wars. The memories of my college days are, not surprisingly, marred by Susan's death, though I look back warmly upon the short time we had together. I owe that to Susan—to recall her with fondness and compassion, dignity. She was my first love, my only love if you must know. I've learned time wants to mitigate the painful and highlight the mirthful. There's a word: mirthful. That's Margaret's word, "a fifty cent-er," she'd say.

How does one begin a game of pain roulette? Pick a photo from the box, any photo, and see where memory takes you. Margaret, always the brave one, reaches her hand into the unknown, gently fingering through the pile of photos like they're rusty fishhooks.

The first photo was taken on a shimmering summer day on a Plum Island, Massachusetts beach. Susan, maybe eight, was wearing a hand-me-down, lime green bathing suit a size too big and barely adhering to her freckled, sunburned shoulders. Her smile is crooked and devious, oversized with gapped front teeth bursting through despite her efforts to tuck them behind reddened lips.

Another, her First Communion. Smile of an angel, her proud father leaning in with his shiny, oily skin, uncomfortable in his church costume, a short, misshapen necktie listing to the left. In another, Susan and Patrick, Christmas morning pajamas, red and green plaids and too tight, probably an aunt's poor estimation as to how much they'd grown in a year. A holiday evergreen looms in the background, the undecorated peak too tall for the room, green branches vining over a length of ceiling like a serpent in wait. Then one where she's in her late teens, close in time to when I met her, beautiful, and already her smile—the one that could melt men's souls—was growing elusive. Patrick, ten years younger and a puff of red curls, stands close to her, unaware a monster lurks in the shadows.

By her late teens, Susan was already sex and curves. Men fawned over her. Women wanted to trade places with her, at least for a moment, just to feel what it was like to command a room without uttering a word. Yet this sway, this ungentle and overwhelming ability to influence others, did not bring her joy. It's this aspect of mental illness that's most confounding to me. How could someone with so many God-given gifts and so many successes not think themselves worthy?

Margaret examines each photo, running her fingertips along the still sharp edges and pointed corners, making little grunts of satisfaction ("hmmmm") before handing them to me. She too is measuring up Patrick, watching the small lines at the edges of his eyes to see if they twitch, attempting to gauge the significance of each photo, each moment the shutter clicked open and shut. Patrick peers out of the corner of his eyes, a gumshoe, never looking directly at us, feigning a study of our modest wall coverings, the dust collected in one corner of the hardwood floor, the low drawl of our neighbor's restless poodle announcing his displeasure with being left outside in the elements. He is almost an apparition, seated with us in our living room but not at the same moment in time, observing from a few feet away, but out of reach. Patrick makes me uncomfortable.

He is different than I remembered, though the last time I'd seen him he was still a child. His red hair has darkened considerably; bits of gray surfaces here and there, like the rest of us. What's his purpose? Forty years on, what is he hoping to uncover under the guise of filling in the gaps of his memory of his beloved sister? Is there something more sinister at work? He's holding something back.

"My only memories of her are when she was sad," Patrick offers while touching two fingers to his lower lip. "I was hoping you could provide something happier, or at least, maybe… less sad."

I can hear Susan in his voice, sultry and rhythmic, yet thoroughly defeated before the day even commenced.

"I've had lots of treatment over the years," he says. "I don't mind telling you. My parents too, though they weren't as severe, well… now, it's just me."

Margaret studies him, her eyes barely slits, chewing her bottom lip. "Hmmmm," she offers, ever the politician.

"I suffer from many of the same demons, you could say, but there are medications now which help, at least somewhat," he continues. "They don't just throw you in a cage anymore."

I take his commentary on cages as an awkward attempt at humor, a self-deprecating endeavor to break the ice, and smile like an idiot. Margaret shoots me a look I can't hope to describe, something from the depths of Hell. I sink deep into the couch, trying to burrow through the velvety, flower print covering to the shoddy foam and springs. I want to strip—shoes, socks, pants, shirt, underwear—and run across the room, leaping smile first through the nearest window, and make my getaway.

"Maybe just *any* memories of Susan," he says after some consideration. He puts on a pair of reading glasses, hipster type—black plastic rims, too small for his face and circular in a John Lennon manner. And his composed demeanor, it's… rehearsed and disingenuous. I wonder what Margaret thinks of him—his smug glasses and Nantucket button down shirt with paisley swirls. She shoots me another glare that makes me shiver.

I have to admit, Patrick has a calming manner and impeccable delivery. He summons your attention while you believe it's your own free will to listen to each carefully honed sentence. Suave would be the right word if forced to choose. Another wasted O'Malley family gift. Such a beautiful and talented family of loonies.

"I'm not sure what I'm searching for, really, everything and nothing. Even little things could be relevant." He laughs at his own words. "Sorry I'm being so vague, I want to paint a picture of Susan, a more complete picture than the one I have now."

He's a liar. And I should know, I've already lied to you. There's not a day goes by that I don't think of Susan. It's just after 10am and I'm stone drunk.

The air in the room grows stale, like the oxygen has been sucked out by a warm, dry wind. The remnants of last night's dinner—rotting broccoli and some kind of fish—escape from the refrigerator and waft into the living room. I think I might puke. In my gin-induced haze, Susan speaks to me. Her voice is soft and inviting, her loving self before the irrational fits and starts. It is the Susan I knew and loved freshman year, before the troubles.

"She called you 'Paddy'." I found my voice. "I just remembered that."

3

What's it like to fuck a ghost? A willing apparition, one that embodies a perfect memory, a perfect point in time, a perfect place—the place where you ceased to question whether your person still exists, whether the person you were once mad about transcends the plane of the living. I'm not sure. But, I do know what it's like to be the other woman, wallowing among the imperfects who still breathe, a hopeless mound of flesh and blood who dare not compete with a memory, who can only wonder if her husband is imagining another each time he extinguishes the lights and greedily reaches across her fading body.

I know Tom drinks.

There's little hints he's been sneaking around, imbibing bits of this and that, choking down an ounce of gin under the guise of a visit to the garage in search of an elusive adjustable wrench or a trek down the narrow basement stairs, flash-light in hand, to check the fuse box which has functioned worry-free for more years than I can count. When he returns from his errand, there are thin cracks in his stoic personality. There is an amusement with trivial things, a slackening of the taut ropes that secure his emotions firmly to the dock. Often times, his face brightens—almost flickers—like Mr. Edison's creation being powered on and off, and his eyes regain an innocent luster and slide slowly across his face, to and fro, like an unwitting pendulum. Most of all, he forgets his troubles, his grey mood, if only for the moment. And for this reason alone, I don't interfere.

Recently, Tom called me an "old soul." What is an old soul, really? Aren't all souls old as time, predisposed and recycled ad infinitum? Or are new ones created independently, seeded and raised for their mortal demise? I don't know, but I do feel like an old soul of late—a rusty gate squealing in pain on a blustery day or the narrow urethra of a leathery old man slowly being strangled by his prostate.

There now, I've cheered myself up a bit with that one!

But perhaps he has a point, old Tom, as the mirror doesn't lie. Though his noticing the condition of my soul, as well as the deepening lines on my face, would seem forty years late. This old soul carries the burden of old thinking, of hunkering down during a storm, of preserving what is necessary to survive lean times and, regrettably, of labeling those I regard as difficult. Yes, I still recall the names we used for people like Susan: disturbed, psychotic, deranged. In our lexicon, this one or that one had suffered a "nervous breakdown" or experienced a "psychotic episode." The milder events—daily fluctuations of mood or cognitive anomalies—were considered negative personality traits. Those, of course, are the old words and the old thinking. The new words, the new thinking, the new treatments came too late for Susan and too late for me.

Patrick's visit was different, however. Even drink could not provide comfort for Tom and I watched him struggle against the tide, attempting to tread water and organize his thoughts only to drift again, lost, slowly drowning. I do believe he wanted to help Patrick bring closure to the mysterious Susan, to unearth the antiquities of her brief existence, but there were limits. I also imagine Tom was sympathetic to Patrick's quest though I'm unsure he was ready to empty his heart. His initial reluctance may have left Patrick wondering if he'd overestimated how willing we might be to help.

Before Susan's brother arrived, prowling our doorstep, parading photographs recovered from his now dead parents' attic, Susan—the thought of Susan—hadn't entered my mind in some years. Now as I lay in bed staring toward the ceiling, she's taken residence in my brain—brilliant green eyes, devil may care wisps of auburn hair bouncing, tiny wrinkles at both corners of her mouth. There was something about her lips. I can't recall exactly, but there was something sincere and sultry. Susan possessed everything I didn't: brains, beauty, grace—and, forty years ago, Tom. She exuded a laugh that made others laugh; made me laugh most. When she cried, sometimes I cried. Often I didn't.

I've already lied to you. She was my best friend and I loved her and not a day goes by when I don't think of her. Of Susan, of Susie, of Sue.

4

I eye Patrick with suspicion—O'Malley auburn hair and Susan's deep green pupils. He even has a couple of dimples that I often hear leading men of Hollywood's golden age possessed, but I've never noticed on a man. And his friendly demeanor—he actually appears like the brother of a girl long dead, aloof and ethereal, alone. And that makes me suspicious.

Not long after we sit in the living room, even before my refreshed cup of coffee has cooled, I rise from my seat and, without excusing myself, walk to the front door and leave the house. I still don't know why. The gin is stowed in a work cabinet in the garage, tucked safely behind a leaking canister of brake fluid, so it isn't for a recharge. I stroll down the brick stairs, over the uneven walkway, cracked and heaved by New England winters, and onto the sidewalk, my bare feet slapping against the cement. The sun is hot on my face, and when I close my eyes, I can see blood red through translucent lids. I immediately begin to perspire. There is a voice from the porch, concern and confusion. Margaret most likely. "Tom?" And "Tom, where are you going?"

The neighborhood itself is unfamiliar even though I've lived there for many years. The tidy grass lawns and sculptured hedges are faded, lying in shadow, fearful of what I've become. Tree leaves above me shake in a light breeze, almost shivering, their once rich green color washed out, ashen and nervous. The songs of the sparrows and robins cavorting in the summer sun, smitten with full stomachs and successful nesting, are unrecognizable and bring me no joy. Even the squirrels, battle-worn and clever from our long-standing war over acorns and birdseed, give me a wide berth.

I lurch across the street, my feet carrying me involuntarily over the sweltering black tar, a puppet being inelegantly maneuvered by some unseen hand shoved up my bottom. It is not a graceful crossing; nothing to be immortalized in oil paint and strung openly in a swanky gallery or museum— how I am able to keep my feet and avoid splitting my face open on the tarmac remains a mystery. A car drives slowly by me, avoiding the train wreck by steering to the left side of the street to pass. A woman in large sunglasses stares cautiously through the tinted window. From the safety of the air-conditioned passenger's seat, she cranes her neck toward me out of either concern or contempt. I waive her away with a dismissive swing of my hand, unsure if she's intent on helping or simply bearing witness to a forthcoming police report.

The house across the street—a parochial, white colonial

with black shutters, a filthy, red brick chimney, black metal mailbox and manicured rose garden—has long stood unchanged, yet I cannot remember where I am or why I'm there. I can see the owner of the house (Mr. Hooper I call him, his actual name escapes me) with his greased flat toupee and pointed, leaking nose, face pressed flat to the kitchen window, his beady eyes—actually, his one good beady eye—fixed on me. His other eye is made of cloudy, off-color glass like a dime store crystal goblet and has a lazy eyelid that droops halfway down, giving the impression he might fall asleep at any moment. He claims the eye (the missing eye) is a war wound suffered during some obscure, forgotten incursion, though I have my doubts.

He's yelling at me or to me, that Hooper, his voice dulled by the panes of glass, both muffled and angry. What is it about Mr. Hooper that I hate? The truth is, I don't hate him—he hates me. And it's for good reason, his hate. I've earned it tenfold.

Over the years, in my quest to become whole, I've dragged down many a victim, or rather, many a willing participant who perhaps carried the same scurrilous weight upon their shoulders. Mr. Hooper and his one good eye could see through me, see my soul and all my ill intentions, my evil deeds, my self-induced and premeditated sicknesses. In other words, I'd hunted down and seduced Mr. Hooper's wife. This is not to say his wife was an innocent and I a vile predator, but I'm not in a position to judge such things.

And what of Mrs. Hooper? That again, is not her real name. It's Johnson or Smith or some other innocuous

European surname, but I know her as Sandra. What led to this unexpected dalliance? For starters, Sandra liked to drink. She was a hider too, a burrower who dug out spaces to hide bottles, backs of cabinets and closets, secret spaces and false fronts, old duffle bags coated in ten years of grey dust. Those were some of my favorites and hers too.

The first time I met her, she was, oddly enough, standing on the same porch as Patrick. She was wearing a smart blue wool business suit, pinstripes, a fitted white blouse with a small white plastic badge with "Sandra—US Census" printed in that official square font reserved for official things. She held a clipboard down low by her thigh like she was no longer fond of it.

When I answered the small, considerate knock on the door, she seemed embarrassed to be standing in front of me. She hid behind a wisp of brown curl that fell across her face and fidgeted with her official ballpoint pen, repeatedly clicking the button like she hadn't yet knocked and was surprised to find someone standing on the opposite side of the door. A handsome woman to be sure, sturdy, with a delicate, blue-veined neck and, even as she forced a smile, delightfully plucky dimples on each side of her face. Under different circumstances, she might be light-hearted and sensitive. At the moment, however, she stood with shoulders hunched forward, silent and forlorn, like someone who was used to being ignored. Her brown hair, other than the uncooperative wisp, was pulled taut from the back and restrained by some sort of metal clip (likely several of them), exposing her forehead and making the rogue brown wisp even more conspicuous. She took in a deliberate, bored breath, heavy and through the nose, before following the official script in a tone befitting a funeral. She'd yet to make eye contact.

"Hi, I'm working for the US Census and was wondering if I could ask you a few questions. Only a few minutes of your time." she said.

"We moved in a few months ago," I interrupted.

"Yes, I know, I've seen you in the yard," she said and blinked several times. I'd disrupted the pace and tone of her by-heart speech. "I actually live in the white house across the street." She may have pointed a finger toward her house, but it was a limp-wristed attempt that painted a clear and dour portrait of her current living arrangement.

In the thick, humid air of May, her pale forehead grew damp with sweat and, despite her efforts to limit her exhales (I assume for my benefit), her breath carried the sweet, metallic scent of cheap vodka. My kind of people.

I pounced. "Can I ask you a question?"

She'd been momentarily detached, thumbing through sheets of white paper on the clipboard with that indifferent, sluggish civil servant flair, but my enquiry raised her left brow and she craned her neck toward me, cartoonish and slightly sad. I could smell the whole of her now as I leaned in to sample the scent of her neck—a hint of guilty Mother's Day perfume and failing deodorant, a sweet and sour intoxicant of a different variety.

"Would you like a drink?" I asked.

She hesitated before answering, her lips parted and eyes grew wide, considering my offer as she sized me up. Her pen had stopped clicking. Was I friend or foe? Had her husband (the soon-to-be-known-as Mr. Hooper) put me up to some shenanigans in the hopes of catching his wife with her hand in the cookie jar, me tempting his beloved with a shirt-polished apple? Or was I simply a kindred spirit, a confidant sans the official uniform and plastic badge, in search of another, like-minded soul. Or (as I implied earlier) was I a predator? Well, yes.

"What did you have in mind?" she asked. It was then I noticed her smile—had it been there the whole time? It was crooked and devious and fantastic. And it was real (the smile), her upper lip unable to contain her slightly off-color canine tooth on one side and her bottom lip bitten firmly between her teeth on the other. Her posture straightened and she pushed away the wisp of curl from the front of her face. There she was, finally, the real Sandra, not the fastidious, meek census taker with the clicking pen. Almost on cue, her hair maneuvered itself out of the clips and fell forward and down her shoulders. Yes, my people indeed.

In time, I found her lips tasted better, silky and metallic, when coated thick with Beefeater gin. She was happy to oblige me this treat, her eyes rolling deep back into her head and her pelvis thrust lustfully each time her arms settled around my neck. There was symbiosis in our liaison: the awakening, the reassurance, the… sordidness. More importantly, I'd converted her from a vodka girl to a gin girl. Two peas in a pod, Sandra and I were full-fledged members of the social class of the lost and forgotten and the often poorly dressed: the drinking class.

We played depraved, non-Census Bureau-sanctioned games like "Find the Pen" and "What Does this Taste Like?" Of the official plastic badge with "Sandra" plastered so innocently across, well, I can only say our actions left it far less innocent.

Around her neck she wore an antique ivory pearl, brownish and opaque, attached to a fragile, crumbling gold chain that could barely hold its weight. She said it was her mother's and her grandmother's and her great grandmother's. It swung wildly in the moment, thumping on her chest like a rogue exterior heartbeat, keeping time. I'd often take it in my mouth and pull gently when she leaned in close. It tasted of metal and earth and family secrets.

"Be careful! If you swallow it, you'll choke on it!"

"And what of it?" I asked. "What if I did?"

"Well," she assured me, "I'd miss you."

"Would I miss myself?" I asked.

"I'd miss you," she whispered and let a ball of spit roll off her tongue and fall into my mouth. "And I'd drink all the gin."

Our census was taken weekly for the better part of three years. I've been led to believe our information on file with the Census Bureau is accurate.

And what of Margaret? What is her knowledge of the situation? Well. Much like my tendency to sneak gin while walking out the trash or sashaying back to check the mailbox for the third time on a rain soaked April afternoon, I do not believe she was aware of my dalliances, at least at the time. Like most men cut from that thread-worn cloth of deceit, those afflicted with that most weighty disease of the mind, I'm careful, you see. I spend my time hiding in plain sight. There have been others, of course.

Now there's pressure in my head, a dull throttling of fuzz. I'm dizzy and stumbling about like an inebriated sailor on a well-earned weekend leave. I remember Hooper's venom rising from his kitchen window podium, the pounding fist on the glass and sill years in the making. He's yelling something about staying away from his wife, her going to live with her sister and almost needing a wheelchair for life, his failing voice muffled by both the glass and the cobwebs in my head. He spews warnings of trespassing and police. I may have smiled at him. I remember my delicate, bare feet being cut raw on Hooper's mangy crabgrass as I shuffled about in circles searching for that hidden pile of tepid dog shit he'd set in wait. I also remember puking in the roses

Margaret and Patrick fish me out of the rose garden, the knees of my tan pants ground black with loam mixed with lawn green, my elbow gritty with blood and shredded white skin. I grunt and spit, yank my arm away from the grip of my rescuers, walk toward… I have no idea. My mouth tastes of sawdust and vintage gin and there is something lodged in my right eye that I attempt (unsuccessfully) to wipe away with my shirtsleeve. There are echoes and grumblings and carrying on, elevated levels of concern (mostly Margaret), and my name called in full throat. I don't answer. Instead, I continue to traipse about Hooper's yard in round, lofty arcs, a fly circling a campfire, before collapsing my weight onto the granite curbstone, my hands slapping my knees as if to say, *Ok, that's enough.*

"Tom. Tom, can you answer me?" asks Margaret, hands flailing about in some kind of perverted semaphore, her mouth slung open and tense. I, her perpetual disappointment, never disappointed.

"Fuck you, Hooper!" I yell over my shoulder and spit again.

"What?" Margaret asks.

"I said 'fuck you' to Hooper. He knows. He knows."

"Can you answer me?" she asks again.

"Yes."

"Are you ok?"

"Yes," I respond. "I'm ok. I may have a bug in my eye."

"You scared me!" she exhales.

I raise my hand to block the sun and look up toward Patrick. He is brooding over me, prowling the tarmac with his perfect green eyes and well-trimmed hair, his debonair and manicured brow, mouth held slightly open, as much confused as concerned. Christ! Does he even have a wrinkle?

"Patrick," I say and swallow the ball of phlegm lodged in my throat, "I didn't kill Susan."

I want him to know.

5

I remember Susan's uncomfortably graphic details of sex with Tom. Like when she told me she could tell what Tom ate for breakfast by the taste of his semen that afternoon. I remember she had an odd way of smoking cigarettes—after all, it was the seventies. When she pulled the glowing white stick from her mouth after a deliberate, elongated inhale, it made a wet, vacuum sound, like someone had snuck up behind her and yanked a lollipop from her lips. Most of all, I remember her troubles.

The truth is, I was always happy when Susan and I were together and sad when we were apart. How simple an assessment. How accurate.

Time has passed me by. Now, where all was once smooth and fair (the corners of my eyes, the pits of my elbows) there are deep lines, odd, unnecessary folds of skin, and the gray hair on my head fights through even the hardiest chemical treatments. The optimist would see it, all of it, as signs of wisdom, but the mirror doesn't peddle in emotion or rationalization. I don't mind aging, but I despise getting old.

People ask if Tom and I were college sweethearts, something outsiders see as a grand story of young love and devotion. We weren't, though we met at Stevens College and, in one form or other, have been together ever since. During our college days, Tom (my Tom) fell for Susan, head over heels.

Do we still use that term: head over heels? Or is there something more fashionable these days? And what of that term—isn't it traditional to have one's head above their heels? Or, when lying down to at least be on an even plane? I'm being coy, of course, but the connotation of head over heels is to be in somersault, flipped about ass over teakettle, turned about in an uncontrolled fashion, disoriented, sick to one's stomach. Was love some twisted, stomach-turning adventure akin to a rusting, poorly maintained carnival ride bumping along at a county fair? That, to me, is a more believable, more practical description; it wrenches your neck and contorts your spine until you're pulverized—even after you've spent earnest money on the ticket. That is love.

Tom and I (yes, Susan's Tom) married thirty-one years ago. As Tom often says, it feels like thirty-two. His sense of humor remains his greatest trait or at least he thinks so. It's very likely I'm the only one who finds him funny. He has always made me laugh. It was my first clue I was attracted to him. Few men (boys when they're young men) are actually funny. We laugh as much at them as with them. They certainly believe they're funny because we continue to laugh and play with our hair, throwing it from one shoulder to the other, moving it aside as it cascades across our faces, wrapping it carefully around our fingers in indelicate foreshadowing. It's all part of the mating ritual yet (at least when we're young) we're the only gender in the know.

There was a boy for me at Stevens. His name was Liam. He was tediously cute with tossed blond curls and a tendency to cater to my every whim. There was nothing wrong with Liam; he was perfectly acceptable. And that was the problem. I had no real interest in him, which, of course, didn't prevent me from leading him on. Yet, in my eyes, there was only Tom, and Tom's eyes always looked past me.

The fact is I enjoyed Liam's company immensely and there were even a few occasions in the dark, humid basement study of the William Lewis Library where, under the guise of proofreading each other's essays, we cocooned (sometimes for hours) in an uncharted corner of carpet and "swapped spit." Forgive the uncouth phrase, but it is an apt description of our endeavors. Upon consideration (and, again, the lens of wisdom), I was attracted to Liam; I must have been. Yet, I did not forgive his transgression on our trip to Cornell—one I had little right to judge, no basis to cast in dank, reprehensible light. But judge I did.

Our college town was—what's that word—quintessential? (That's a real fifty-cent-er!) Yes, a quintessential Massachusetts college town and it still is to this day. There were used bookstores and quaint pubs, red brick sidewalks and map shops, stately Victorians perched high on hills overlooking sun-drenched, grassy commons. There were several obscure museums in the town, each honoring benefactors of the college, and carefully preserved homes where time-darkened oil paintings of reluctant family members stood guard over path-worn wool rugs and furniture carved with intricate patterns imported from far-flung places.

Who could resist the intoxicating smell of Lombardi's Bakery, the wait line spilling onto the sidewalk and extending halfway down the block, or a greasy slice of pizza from Steve's at Stevens? Adding edginess to the local culture, there were also drunken students urinating in sidewalk planters on Friday nights and occasional fights with townies—longstanding, generational grudges over girls long forgotten.

Autumn was a glorious time at Stevens, the air cool and crisp with the sweet scent of apples, the tree leaves showing their quality in red, orange and yellow while working through their annual striptease. The yellow and black wasps were beside themselves that time of year, worked into a heavy lather as the ticking seasonal clock brought their time to a close. The pimple-faced freshman, confused and sheepish, nervously crossed streets, refusing to ask directions or accept being lost.

What else can I conjure up about Stevens? Great iron gates, twisted sentinels lording over cobblestones and rain-darkened pathways, gas lamps retrofitted in disappointing electric light casting damp, mottled shadows. The nights, dark and cool, silent, save the clicking of heels on the cobble and echoes of laughter, carefree voices rising and falling. The mornings—I remember them most. November in Massachusetts, the taste of the warming air, dry and sour in my mouth, the swoosh of fallen leaves kicked upward with each step, the sun oddly angled after the autumn equinox, beaming through the clouds between buildings, gently kissing my face.

The William Lewis Library at Stevens College was as old as time, white cement base and sun-dulled red brick, translucent leaded windows, panes assembled into small squares and weathered bluish-green, austere in the daylight like someone taking their last breath. It was, and still is, my favorite building. Like most buildings at Stevens, it was endowed with those slithering ivy vines, untamed yet somehow perfectly coiffed. The buildings along the admissions tour route especially were graced with this ivy (not an accident I suspect), meant to encourage post-tour conversation at suburban dinner parties where men in starched oxford shirts compared investment portfolios and thin women with straight shoulders bragged about their little brats and tennis clubs.

What about my fellow students? I recall a gray, mousey girl with straight, dirty blond hair and a thin, whistling nose who undressed the fraternity boys on Saturday night, then spent Sunday elaborating upon the church sermon the rest of us had slept through. And the sleepy, freckled boy with eyes set deep into his skull, a closet vegetarian who stared uncomfortably long at Susan, all the while refusing to face his sexuality for fear of Daddy cutting off his tuition. I often wonder what became of those two and if they knew that I knew their secrets.

More than my classes, I remember the walks to class. I grew up during those walks—Susan working a cigarette, holding court, Tom hanging on her every word, me, mostly listening, laughing, living. I remember Susan describing what she would do with (and to) Professor Somebody, a handsome, plaid-jacketed political science professor. Then, Tom frowning, Liam wondering aloud where he could purchase a similar plaid jacket. Was she joking? Difficult to say; I never asked—it was more fun to just believe she would.

I remember Liam's gentle kiss on the back of my neck and goosebumps. I remember Susan and Tom lost in each other's eyes. I remember Tom and Liam whispering something about Susan's tight, powder blue sweater. I remember smiles. I remember Susan throwing off her shoes and wading through the wet morning grass. I remember being friends for a hundred years after knowing each other for a month. I remember gazing toward the waning autumn sun as it heated my freckled face, squinting, shaking my head in mock disbelief, pondering if life could ever be better.

Well before the flowers of spring, we were inseparable, the four of us in a blind, giddy lockstep over red bricks on our journey to... anywhere. The semester break for Christmas and shared letters home (windy and juvenile) only served to strengthen our bond, my stomach aching in wait for the postman to arrive each day and, ultimately, the turn of the calendar signaling our return to campus.

On the way to Stevens, there was a little ice cream shop

around a small bend of Route 133, an innocuous white shack in winter, purple awning rolled tight against the roof's overhang, the windows boarded shut for the season. In season though, it was a hornet's nest of activity. The sight of the shop was a delightful landmark and meant we were most of the way to campus. Directly across the street stood a weathered gasoline station, woefully out of place, complete with a squat, blue-shirted proprietor, skin around his finger-nails impossibly stained with grease, who stood (maybe for hours), windshield cleaner and rag at the ready.

My father's blue Plymouth Fury (the pride of the sev-enties, too big for the road and grossly overpowered for our use) hummed forward effortlessly, my father's thick, black-rimmed glasses and bushy, gray-flecked moustache filling the entirety of the rearview mirror. He craned his neck when we passed the gas station, the heavy lenses worth the extra expense, reading the faded red sign perched atop two rusty polls. "58 Cents," he said to himself as fathers do. "Not bad." In my experience, the ever-thirsty Plymouth was required to fill-up at each and every gas station without fail—some longstanding natural law of internal combustion—but we drove straight past the 58-cent-er with complimentary windshield clean. From the concourse-sized backseat, my relief was well-hidden. There wasn't five minutes to waste!

The first time we passed the ice cream shop, it was a Saturday morning, late August or early September. A wind-ing, lopsided queue of customers paralyzed the parking lot. Loud, giddy tourists on day drives dressed in summer whites mixed uneasily with locals, hands on their hips, sporting flannel shirts in anticipation of Thanksgiving. My father gave the line a thorough once-over as the Plymouth slowed, his mouth slightly open and moustache twitching. My mother weighed in with a drawn out "Noooo." This was the only other time I can remember a longstanding natural law being broken: my father and ice cream. For me, this first trip carried much different feelings than I expected: anxiety, fear, perhaps even regret at having agreed to the journey—I didn't really want to get there. There were too many unknowns.

Not surprisingly, my father wanted to "have a look see" when we arrived at Stevens. My mother—gaudy, oversized white plastic sunglasses from Filene's, heavy, red lipstick and a fresh perm—agreed, twisting her body in the front seat to face me as I cowered in the back, her tight curls bouncing across her cheek before springing back into place. "Do you mind if we drive around and look at the town?" I said I didn't mind. Had I known I would soon become an unlikely expert on every obscure museum in town, I would have opted for a long wait in line followed by a medium-sized Rocky Road stuffed into a sugar cone.

As for our social (as my mother called our group of friends while breathing through a formidable cloud of Chanel No. 5 and Virginia Slims), our friendship blossomed upon our return to campus. Before January's end, Susan and I began whispering "I love you" each time we reluctantly parted, arms extended toward the other, fingers stretched to breaking, fingertips touching until the last possible moment. When reunited at last, our day's itinerary fulfilled, we hugged like favorite cousins long separated by holidays, wondering aloud who missed each other more. Tom and Liam were overjoyed. They bathed in this unexpected, free-flowing affection whenever possible, stealing quick gropes and damp tongue kisses, cupping Susan's ass with greedy palms. Being felt-up several times a day became almost normal, nearly as commonplace as brushing my teeth. And, to be clear, the boys weren't the only ones groping. Silly and innocent, perhaps. Irresponsible and forbidden, yes—I loved it all!

Predictably and sadly, this moment in time, like so many things we cherish, proved fleeting and, as fate would score it, ultimately devastating. The sweet scents and warm yellow sunshine of spring peeking through budding branches, the New England countryside bursting in rebirth and regeneration ushered in unambiguous warnings, unpleasantness so tempestuous and profound, it's impossible to imagine we were blind to its machinations. How could we have overlooked the signs, so very obvious, when we were living on each other's laps, breathing each other's air, perpetually mouthing each other's tongues?

The answer is ugly and grotesquely simple: we were acutely aware of Susan's decline and chose to do nothing. We were too busy enjoying ourselves and the fruits of our youth—using the void of weekends to ply ourselves with alcohol and chemicals while lustfully pawing each other's bodies—to allow melancholy to become the enemy of mirth, sailing too fast for an unscheduled dip in the wind to slow the voyage. In the moment, it was vastly more important to have a firm grip on Susan's ass than keep a steady hand on Susan herself. It must have been this way. I have nothing other than some vague, translucent memories of so many of these events while others are so clear, the conversations burned verbatim into my memory.

"Where the hell is Tom?" she asked one day while eating lunch in the cafeteria. "I told him one o'clock. Can the man even tell time? He's an idiot!"

"He'll say he didn't wind his watch," I said, referring to one of the devilish tricks of men, the feigning of ignorance. I could picture it, Tom's boyish and indignant half-smile as he attempted to deflect her vitriol and, despite the demeaning odds, remain in love with the fiend.

She briefly considered my theory. Then, she shifted moods and inquired about my love life (my "lust life" she called it), lit a cigarette and promptly pulled the lollipop from her mouth.

She asked about this one and that one from my dorm, my Psych class. The names and memories of them, mostly escape me. She asked about Liam, too. Despite my insistent truth that Liam and I were merely friends, she could not contain her interest, leaning forward with an inexplicable grin, tooth and gums, before releasing a tightly formed stream of smoke toward the ceiling.

Reflecting back, there was surely some small lie or at least an expansion on a truth I could have invented to satisfy the moment, some semblance of debauchery to entertain my eager audience. I was never the thespian, not one to build upon the mildest event, transforming and bending it until it reached a seething, breathtaking conclusion. I simply lacked the imagination for such things. Thus, with nothing for me to report, Susan settled back into her seat, dejected and disappointed, as always.

Susan would have invented something—some elaborate, unexpected and disgustingly fantastic yarn. One story she shared (true or invented, I'll never know) involved an English professor, a windy fellow with proper brown leather brogues, a weathered, overstuffed briefcase and thin, wire-rimmed glasses. Her dilemma: a failing grade acquired through earnest avoidance of almost any academic pursuit whatsoever. As she eloquently described it, she'd "earned the failure." A trip to his office—a dull, sooty place that matched his demeanor—resulted in both under the desk fellatio and the awarding of three credits.

"I know what men want," she said and rolled her eyes upward, deep into her skull and burst into her intoxicating laugh.

Tom never arrived at lunch—not an unforgivable slight, but certainly not recommended considering Susan's growing unpredictability. She took it in stride.

"He probably just forgot," she said and rolled her shoulders upward. "That's my Tom," she concluded with a thin smile, fingering a wisp of hair away from her eyes as she rose from the table. I can't recall his excuse for missing lunch, but he'd been granted a reprieve. One more day.

Over time, Susan's behavior became a ridiculous and extravagant false accent, too absurd and insufferable to be real. At first, we were entertained by it, her quirky mood swings and inability to filter her thoughts, her inability to distinguish between what should be shared and what should be buried in a hole or at least stated in private. Did this embolden her to continue on with the farce or were we missing obvious signs? To us, it was sport, a bit of entertainment, would she or wouldn't she? We were suspicious of her mental state, but also morbidly curious. Would she berate Tom for the mildest indiscretion, verbally undress him, leaving him mouth slung open and emotionally nude, emasculated for all the world to see? Or would she build him up with compliments and affection, leaving him beaming like a fool, all white teeth and tussled hair, even more in love with her than yesterday? From which side of the bed had she risen this morning? Were we to endure Susan the self-centered bitch or the kinder, more jovial and fun loving Susie? Or perhaps the amalgamation of the two: Sue. Susan, Sue or Susie? How could I balance my love and hate? Over time, as the small paper cuts of Susan's malice began to fester, I wanted to drag her limp carcass down into the reeking swamp mud on the far side of campus. But I loved her too much.

The 1970's were not a time to be saddled with disease of the mind. At our most impressionable age, society was resolutely unequipped for the realities of mental illness, unwilling to treat sufferers as anything more than social deviants, wretched outcasts better shunned and marginalized then treated with compassion. We, like society, took up a broom and raised the corner of a throw rug, sweeping inconvenience and abnormality underneath. Forty years later, we (Tom and I) are still digesting our role in all of it, though it's not something we discuss. It just exists in the air we breathe, a subtle odor indicating something unsavory is buried under the floorboards.

The word guilt is insufficient, though it's a remarkably practical word that I find difficult to improve upon. A bare palm bearing down on a searing cast iron skillet would be considerably closer to what haunts me, yet still falls short. Even now, almost nightly, my unoiled mind seizes and coughs, sputters, punishes me anew, abandoning any half-baked justification, tearing down whatever asinine theory I've concocted over the measure of a day. Then, deserted by sleep, I reconfirm this—all of it—can't be undone. There are natural laws that—even provided my father's nimbleness—do not present opportunity to be broken. Time past is unalterable, fate's covenant cannot be renegotiated. Ghosts remain ghosts.

In early May, as finals loomed, we embarked on a road trip, the first, and last, of my college career. We agreed I'd pick Susan up at eleven, have a bite to eat, then begin the already regrettable, six-hour drive to Cornell. Allegedly, Liam's brother (a worldly fraternity senior whose name escapes me) had scored us tickets to the Grateful Dead show in Ithaca, New York. Penny store maps, ill-folded against the grain and well-inked with blue ballpoint pen arrows and unbalanced circles, were at the ready, along with cigarettes, a warm six-pack of Pepsi, a warmer case of Narragansett, assorted potato chips, duly crushed and stale, and child-sized,

Cub Scout sleeping bags lifted from the musty basement of Liam's parent's house. Lastly, Liam, following guidance from his brother's book of shady contacts, procured some pills, small white tablets of acid. Were we to sleep in the car or some vomit-floored frat house? It mattered not at that age. The tickets (the carrot dangled on a stick and string) were our golden prize for the plodding, miserable run we were voluntarily undertaking and Liam kept reminding us of this fact, keeping us motivated.

The afternoon prior, we cobbled together money for gas and not much else, emptying our pockets of jumbles of nothingness (mostly coins, lint and string) into the middle of our cafeteria table, each committing to the weekend as a commune. It was a practical lesson in economics for a handful of idiots operating on the fringes of a functional economy. As I counted the currency in my head, poking about the pile with my finger in hopes one of the silver-colored coins would turn out to be gold, Susan (ever the mother of invention) hatched a plan.

While in the cafeteria, Susie instructed us to lift whatever food not nailed down: slices of bread, rolls, butter; paper lunch bags filled with cereal; leaky, red and white elementary-school-sized cartons of milk one day past the expiration date. Liam floated about willy-nilly, a specter in a black t-shirt, plucking this and that from here and there. We thought ourselves quite sly, slippery thieves, barely containing high-pitched giggles and nose-wetting snorts as we breached the exit.

The cafeteria staff—tired, white-hatted women in

combat-heavy, white cotton aprons and retired army types with crew cuts and blue ink tattoos—barely raised an eye to our brazen daylight raid. In all likelihood, the yawning staff, weeks from pension, intentionally overlooked our pilferage and simply assumed it to be another cheeky, orchestrated prank for beer-addled Greek pledges.

And what of Tom? What role would he play in this descent disguised as a pilgrimage, this whorish red lipstick squeamishly applied to a pig? If memory serves (which it may not), an invitation was put forth, but Tom wisely decided against twelve bumpy hours trapped in Liam's father's air conditioning-free Dodge Dart sandwiching a concert he had no interest in attending. The seductive lure of the car's 8-track player and its promise of near angelic quality sound apparently fell on deaf ears. Or were there only three tickets awaiting us at Cornell? Is it possible Liam was more cunning than expected?

By now, small changes had come to our quartet. For several weeks, Tom was distant, preoccupied with something else, an asterisk or sidebar that remains a mystery. While Liam grew more confident, Tom slowly developed an eerie, unbecoming silence. He began to hone his new skill in Liam's presence, long pauses and deliberate exhales following passive-aggressive questions or comments, like he was allowing the three of us time to process and digest his intent. Things like, "Of course, some of you would know that if…" Yes, his measured needling boiled Susan's blood.

"What the fuck?" Susan blurted out after one of Tom's petulant, verbal fits. "Does he think I can read his mind? I don't like games."

"I think he's jealous."

"Jealous?" The word seemed foreign to her, a paradox.

"Of Liam."

Susan's eyes rolled backward and her jaw grew rigid, her lips pulled thin, emptying them of color. "What's his problem? He knows I love him. What else does he need to know?"

"Boys are weak," I offered and waived a snarky, dismissive hand. "Emotionally fragile. In need of constant validation. Should I go on?"

"Assholes."

"Sure, that too."

She crunched up her nose and forehead, top teeth resting on her bottom lip and shook her head, her shoulders pulled upward, a blend of disgust and indignation with light sprinkles of guilt. "What does he think I see in Liam? I mean, he's…Liam."

"He does stick his tongue in your mouth."

She broke into her best Susie laugh, the giggling, snorting, gorgeous sound I still hear in my sleep. "Yes," she agreed, "There is that. So does everyone else!"

Susie was so casual about sex, something I could never master. It's no wonder Tom was jealous—not of sex, per se, but of her sexuality, the erotic gravitational pull of her being, her fragrant, natural scent akin to a bitch in heat. And, to be clear, it wasn't simply a physical attraction—it was all of her. She made everything more fun, emotions more intense. Even old men were renewed in her presence, thin fellows in well-worn paddy caps and plaid shirts, and bald, over-fed types with oily beards, all fell over themselves to have a look, intent on chasing the intoxicating scent one last time before death's waiting thumb snuffed then out.

One might think the tongue-wagging admirers, young and old, parading about your girlfriend would promote a prideful arrogance, but as Tom was well aware, his relationship with Susan (all relationships with Susan) balanced on the razor's edge, subject to her fickle whims and wildly oscillating moods. It could end or begin in an instant. We all understood this. It was Susan's covenant. But none, as I would learn, were more aware than Liam.

The trip to the concert did not begin or end as expected.

Like most freshman dorms, Susan's room was a joyless void, a rectangular closet with two low slung beds covered in patchwork comforters and yellowed pillowcases, deliberately empty walls and stale, warm air that barely stirred even when the only window was thrown wide open. The fluorescent ceiling light gave the room a peculiar bluish-green hue and hummed incessantly like it was still thinking of an answer to some question asked months ago. The floor too was depressing and old-fashioned, the flaking tile (white with flecks of black and brown) was more suited for the basement of a Civil War hospital.

Often, her chain-smoking, mid-western roommate, Becky or Betsy—a lanky, studious type with straight, unwashed brown hair and brownish-red freckles—occupied the room. She sat in the same corner for hours, on the floor, back to the wall, legs in an impossible pretzel, pads of her bare feet darkened and calloused, her frayed jeans stained from lunch. Nearby, an overflowing black ashtray threatened to topple over. From this position, Becky or Betsy played the flute while writing uninspired Beat poetry and assembling million-piece jigsaw puzzles of Vermont covered bridges and Himalayan kittens. She was boring and parochial and spoke out of one side of her mouth. I never saw her use the bathroom.

Becky or Betsy ran with an odd crowd of misanthropes, radicals and future accountants who dressed in professor tweed and, apparently, saw little value in personal hygiene. They often sat near, or rather around, Becky, endless clouds of smoke choking out the bluish-green light, creating a poet-friendly atmosphere. There was always a pungent odor encircling the group, an unpleasant swirl of wet cheese and warm low tide. Liam, with his ridiculous laugh, cruelly referred to their group as "The Guess the Smell Gang."

It was odd that no one answered the door that morning. No Becky. No Betsy. No Susan, No Guess the Smell Gang. The room wasn't overly large so my knock couldn't have gone unnoticed and I thought it unlikely Becky had gone to the bathroom. I knocked again, this time with more determined sass, skinning my knuckles on the rough paint. I leaned my ear to the door. Nothing. There was no joyful singing or baleful sob, just silence. My mind wandered, of course—she knew I was coming around eleven. That was our last conversation. I was sure there was no confusion. My ear stuck to the tacky paint as I pulled away. I tried to wipe away whatever paint might still be clinging to my ear like I was shooing a fly.

The hall was empty save the clicking of my shoes on the tile and my own imagination. I walked down the hall to the girl's bathroom, a humid box with white tiled walls and leaky pipes crisscrossing the ceiling. All of it reeked of stale cigarettes and moldy drains. There were three rust-stained sinks (drain stops on brownish chains hung over the sides), three bathroom stalls installed the previous century, and two shower areas carved into the walls, their entrance ways covered by thin, yellow, mold-stained shower curtains.

"Susan?" I called from the entryway while trying not to touch anything. My voice echoed back to me. The bathroom appeared to be empty.

A girl with grey teeth and frizzy red hair tried to squeeze past me and into the bathroom. She was wearing a blue terrycloth robe with white trim and carried a basket of assorted toiletries. It was nearly noon and she was barely conscious, bouncing off me into the wall, using it to steady herself. I'd seen her around the dorm on several occasions, but never had the occasion to speak with her. Though perpetually detached, she always appeared vaguely friendly or, at least, not unfriendly. She was one of Becky's poet friends, a fellow kitten puzzler, so I found her hurried stagger toward the shower, though welcome, to be slightly out of character.

"Have you seen Susan?" I asked.

She looked past me, staring blankly as if trying to determine where she'd seen me before. She wiped the sleep out of her eyes. It's possible she was disappointed or even annoyed that I had no real interest in speaking with her. "Ummm… no. Maybe this morning? I'm not sure." Her voice echoed then trailed off.

"You saw her this morning?"

"Maybe. I haven't had coffee yet, so, I really don't know." Though we were at the entrance to a windowless room, she raised a hand like she was shielding her face from the morning sun, her eyes pulled tight to a squint and her nose crunched upward.

"Ummm… did you check her room?" she asked and tilted her head to one side.

I paused, unsure of her level of seriousness.

"No, I hadn't thought of that." I answered.

"Well, that's where I'd start."

We stood there for a few moments staring at each other, her nodding, both wondering why the other had chosen to waste their time. After a minute, I surrendered, moving aside to let her pass, the wall guiding her way as she slid by, toiletries hugged close to her body and at the ready.

In time, I've come to realize our mocking ways, our references to "The Guess the Smell Gang" and the like, the collective turning up of our noses, the thought of being their betters was not a well-kept secret. There were many evenings when, plied with alcohol or worse, we spoke openly, our voices brimming with unearned arrogance, without the benefit of sobriety's filter and with complete disregard for the feelings of those around us (the collateral damage). We were untouchable, floating in our own insulated and ethereal world that revolved around Susan, our brilliant private sun. Everyone else who existed in our universe occupied some pock-marked and churlish moon, craggy and shadowed, destined to spend eternity held in check by our gravitational pull, never to arrive. This callous thoughtlessness would hardly be the only example of our—my—burgeoning immaturity. Soon I would make the worst mistake of my life, a disgusting, life-altering blunder so self-serving that it would cost us our sun, casting us into perpetual darkness.

As I approached Susan's door for the second time, I unconsciously wiped at my ear, nervously clearing away phantom germs and viruses and grime. It was the first time I considered that something might be off, a premonition. My body heated and I began to sweat. A rumble of panic, thus far unfounded, worked its way from my feet up through the tips of my fingers. I wiped at my damp forehead with the back of my wrist. I stood at the door for what felt like several minutes, staring at the black painted room number—five—unable to raise my hand to knock.

Now there were girls in the hallway, shuffling back and forth, their heels clicking and voices raised, doors opening before closing with a thud, creating a vacuum of air that popped in my ears. The dorm was reborn at the stroke of noon as hangovers waned and empty stomachs began to ache. They milled about in makeshift heather grey pajamas and baggy, boy's sweatshirts, smoking in small semi-circles like someone had just invented it, a thick blue cloud hung just below the ceiling. Some used the payphone to call Mom and Dad, providing a progress report on their grades while asking them to send a few dollars, or to calm worried boy-friends at far away universities or left behind at home to wait and wonder. Others rushed to the bathroom with face cloths and worn toothbrushes hoping to claim one of the suddenly scarce shower stalls.

There were several boys too, wrinkled clothes and tus-sled hair, sneaking their way toward the prison wall with ladders and shovels while the penitentiary guards were between shifts. I could feel them, all of them, staring at the back of my head, the poor girl, alone in the world, standing at attention in front of a closed door. Some of them may have said hello, I'm not sure if I answered back.

I closed my eyes tight, then raised my hand and knocked. "Susan?"

A small voice replied, dreamy and far away, like a stuffed toy bear whispering to me in my sleep: "I'm here."

I turned the doorknob—it was unlocked—and pushed the door open slowly. The yellow noontime sun cascaded through the window, briefly blinding me and casting the room's lone figure in a vague, blurred silhouette. After this day, if I were asked to depict death, to draw a humanized representation of the wretched thing, I believe I could. It took a moment for my eyes to adjust to the light. Susan, her physical being, swayed in the center of the room, ensnared in some purgatory, oscillating somewhere between falling down and not falling down.

Her hands covered her face and her legs almost buck-led. There was blood near the front pockets of her blue jeans, smeared in brownish crescents, ironic smiling cartoon mouths. Red still bubbled from her wrists and knuckles, forming small streams of crimson that ran down her fore-arms and pooled in the soft, shallow pits of her elbows. I couldn't speak. The room reeked of curdled blood and dampness and something sad. Despite my previous assump-tions that the floor, flecks and all, would camouflage any stain or spill, it could not contain the scarlet of blood. There were small, single droplets, here and there, larger ones where she'd paused for a moment, and thick, barefooted smears in brilliant, maniacal patterns. It didn't look like a slaughter, no violent struggles or bloodthirsty madness, but rather a slow, steady leak, a hairline crack in the dam. Looking back, that's exactly what it was, a slow leak, a car tire slowly wearing down over months and years, nearly imperceptible, until, at the worst possible moment, it fails, stranding everyone on board on a snowy, rural interstate in the middle of the night.

Now, Susan's eyes were clear and bright. Whatever sad-ness or perhaps, madness, had overtaken her, now released its grip. I grabbed a towel from a dresser drawer, littering the floor with whatever other clothing it contained, then pushed her arms together and wrapped the towel tightly around the cuts on her wrists. I walked her to her bed and sat down next to her. She didn't resist.

"I just wanted see how it felt," she said and almost laughed, her eyes focused on Betsy's unoccupied corner. "I wanted the pain, to feel the pain. See what it was like. Just for a moment."

"Did it hurt?" I asked.

"A little," she replied. "I wasn't trying to hurt myself. I

mean really hurt myself. Why are you crying?"

"I don't know," I said. "You scared me, I guess."

"I'm not scared," she said and confidently shook her head.

I looked around the room, unsure what I was expecting to find.

"What… ummmm… what did you use?" I asked.

"Scissors. Over there, on the desk."

"Jesus."

"Thing is sharp," she laughed. "But I didn't get very far."

"You got far enough. Let me look."

"Just a lot of blood, really. It's nothing. I'm sure it looks worse than it is. It always looks worse than it is."

When I removed the towel, I thought I might throw up. Yes, I'd heard of cutting one's wrist, the act itself, violent, sometimes, masochistic, but to see the resulting trench, to smell the mangled flesh and sour metal of blood, to witness the seeping crimson, freshly raked to the surface, to hold the result of this violence in my hand, terrified my soul.

If she could read my reaction to the carnage I witnessed, she hid it well. The poor, beautiful fool!

"See," she said, her voice calm and dismissive, her head tilted to one side, hair falling over her face, there was even a quick, devious smile, like she was posing for a snapshot on an innocuous spring afternoon.

"Not bad at all. I told you."

Were the calls of her demons satisfied and a degree of relief achieved? Yes, it appeared so. For the moment at least, Susan had returned. She'd driven toward the cliff at unsustainable speed and slammed the brakes, skidding to the edge, perhaps staring over into the abyss, but came to rest safely short of disaster.

Though I was blind to it at the time, this was the first of the two defining moments of my life. As fate would hold, both involved Susan, but neither was of her making—they were mine and mine alone. Such weighty things should not be pressed upon the narrow shoulders of the young. The young are impulsive and fearless, confident and emotional, impervious, and above all, selfish. The word "overly" could be placed in front of each of those descriptions. It's why the young are sent to war while fat old men plan and scheme from the safety of climate-controlled cement bunkers. I see that now. But during those halcyon days at university, that time of enlightenment to the ways of the world, when I held Susan's wrists, torn and leaking, what did I do?

If we mitigate the gray of thought and judgment and peer through a lens of purely black and white, there were two choices: call an ambulance and get her medical attention and ideally, psychiatric help, or make light of it and save my weekend plans—meaning bandage her up and make our way to Cornell. It was a simple choice of selfish versus unselfish, responsible citizen versus deviant, the now versus the future. Yet, there was no choice, no tricky moral dilemma, no paradoxes to ponder—there was someone in immediate danger. And it was not just someone, it was Susan, a sister to me, my best friend, my love. But a choice was made—one of a hundred choices I've made each day for sixty years, a determinist's potpourri of poor decisions and uneducated guesses, many worse than others.

In the end, I convinced myself she was right; it really wasn't that bad. She'd experienced a momentary lapse of judgment, a slip up, a blip, a hormone-fueled peak of raw emotion. Harmless. I'd have Liam drive me to the drug store to purchase some medical tape and bandages. She'd be ship-shape in no time at all. None the worse for wear. Brand new.

I'd left the door to room number five slightly open, a crack wide enough for the curious to stick their nose through. A thin, musky girl in a red plaid mini skirt and heavy heels was peering in. Her curiosity unsettled me and I rose to secure the door. The girl (curls and dark hair, I forget her name too) asked if Susan was "ok," but I squeezed her question out as she spoke, her voice fading off.

"Is Susan alright?" she asked again as the door cut her off from the room, pushed back into the piss-yellow hall-way. There was someone lurking behind the musky girl, a blue robed blur, spying over and around her like a salivating dog, curious also of Susan's current condition. It was the redhead from the bathroom. I imagine she was not entirely displeased.

Piss—that was our name for the dull yellow paint cover-ing the cinderblock walls of our dorm. And it wasn't just the dorm, the walls of several buildings on campus were coated in the horrible stuff. "Take a left at the piss" was not an uncommon element in a set of directions. At some point, it's likely a thrifty building manager had been offered a deal, a budget-friendly purchase of bulk interior paint, piss yellow, a decade's worth in great overflowing barrels, a bargain too good to pass up. I don't know what made me think of that.

"Where's Becky?" I asked.

"Betsy. Home for the weekend."

"Do you want something to eat?"

"Sure, I could use something. We can go to the cafeteria."

"Why don't you stay here and rest. I'll get you a sandwich or something."

"I'm fine, really."

"Just stay here and keep your wrists pressed against the towel to make sure the bleeding has stopped. I'll be back in a few minutes."

Once I closed the door behind me, I dug though my purse and found a dime for the pay phone. I was hyperventilating, the weight of the moment finally catching up. I called Liam's floor. A boy answered and for a moment thought it was a prank call since heavy breathing was a common element those days. Once we established it was a serious phone call, he was able to track down Liam within a few minutes. I instructed Liam to take some of our trip money and drive to the local pharmacy for some witch hazel, medical pads and white tape and bring it to Susan's room.

"Ok, Can I ask why?"

"Susan had an accident."

"An accident? Is she ok?"

"I think so, for now."

"What does that mean? Are we still going?"

"It means you ask too many questions!" I hung up the phone and went to the cafeteria.

Why did I call Liam instead of Tom? I've often wondered what drove my decision. For practical reasons, Liam had access to a reliable automobile and could, therefore, make the run to the pharmacy in reasonable time. Liam also made logical sense—compared to Tom, he was emotionally detached and unlikely to pass judgment, accepting whatever plausible explanation I would concoct and leaving it at that. Now, the truth of the matter is Liam could be manipulated. I was keenly aware of his fondness for Susan. I could take advantage of this adolescent crush, knowing he would drop everything, regardless of importance, even leave a warm meal on the table and rush to Susan's aid whatever the circumstances.

As I would soon learn, for Liam, this weekend was the culmination of a sinister plan, the payoff, the cracking open of the bank vault after weeks of reconnaissance, of watching the scheduled movement of the security guard and the predictable patterns of the fastidious bank manager. He understood every variable and every potential obstacle. I was not specifically aware such a plan existed, only that it was imperative Susan traveled with us. Of this, he was transparent like all boys of that age, the way they prowl about chest thrust forward, drooling like fools, sniffing and baring their teeth, like a fox scouting a henhouse. This little bump in the road, Susan's episode, in the end, did little to prevent the achievement of his goal.

It was also true that Tom, rather than travelling to Cornell, chose to remain back on campus under the questionable guise of studying, writing this or that paper. Perhaps he was intent on bedding a fellow inmate while the warden was on holiday or at least setting some sordid wheels in motion for future gain. But—as much as I secretly desired their break-up—there was a different reason I wouldn't have called him that day. Susan, all of her, inspired a cult-like following. She was revered as a deity and we followed her with pious conviction. I didn't want to alter that devotion for Tom. I didn't want him to see her in a weakened state, at her most vulnerable for fear she would fall from grace. Maybe being exposed to her in a moment of weakness would serve to cement her regal status, allow her to be seen as someone who can overcome all. It's possible, but I wasn't willing to take that risk. The dynamic of our group required our unwavering worship and willingness to withstand both her kindness and her cruelty. Her personality and her mind, as well as her physical traits, were the glue.

In the cafeteria, there were two grilled cheese sandwiches, squished flat and burned on the edges—and I was lucky to get them. The sleepy and bored cashier, hair pulled tight into a bun on top of her head with cheese breath, greeted me with: "You'd better hurry. We're not supposed to let anyone in after twelve-thirty." There were a handful of other students milling about, taking their last bites of tepid Salisbury steak and tater tots, some still clearing the sleep from their eyes. I hurried through to the cooler area, my shoes tapping and sliding, echoing on the tile. I found two small cartons of milk, the last of their kind, and a small bag of potato chips. Along with the grilled cheese, it was all I could gather in my haste to return to the dorm before Liam.

Susan was sleeping on top of the covers, flat on her back, arms by her sides. I gently checked her wrists. The bleeding had stopped, leaving wads of blood, dried and scabbed. A cursory glance at the bedding didn't reveal any reddish stains. Her breathing, yes, I checked to make sure there was breathing. It was slow and deep with a small whistle, the sleep of someone who hadn't slept in a week. There had never been reason to take notice of Susan's skin color and I found it an odd task to take notice of it now—pinkish-white. While I couldn't be sure what shade she was yesterday or, for that matter, the day before, I was fairly certain pinkish-white was far better news than a shade of blue.

I sat in her desk chair and placed the makeshift lunch on the desk. There was nothing to do now but wait for her to awaken and gauge her mood, take the temperature of her mental state. It was like a fairytale, all eyes on the beautiful princess as she slept, lips puckered for only a true prince's kiss, each cycle of breath, stomach rising and falling, met with undue anticipation—would she awaken rejuvenated, delighting her servants with grace and compassion, a celebrated return to the kingdom, or did the wicked Queen of Scissor, the twisted usurper of sanity, drain away her life essence with a slash, leaving behind a despondent, empty vessel?

My fingers picked at one of the now cold grilled cheese, taking tiny, bird bites between my index finger and thumb and popping them into my mouth. The taste of butter and grease, burnt bread, was a welcome distraction. Then the chips, more grease and a heavy dose of salt. I chewed lightly to dull the sound. My fingernails were next, I chewed them jagged and down to the skin, bloodied. Each tick of my watch echoed throughout the room, ringing in my ears, a minute, sixty ticks, plodded along, answering to no one, hurried by none. Pacing the room achieved little other than to elevate my anxiety.

Somewhere in the hallway there was a shuffling of feet. It wasn't the confident, efficient steps of a female, small click-clacks in quick succession, but rather the elongated, lazy scrapes of a male—the sound of someone reluctantly moving toward somewhere. The noise gave me reason to investigate, a reason to lift myself from the chair and pull my fingernail out from between my teeth. Liam arrived sometime after one o'clock, his color leaned toward a concerned pale. I met him in the hallway. He was carrying a paper bag from the pharmacy in one hand, the other hand was buried in the pocket of his jeans.

"Were you able to get everything?" I asked.

"Yes. What the fuck in going on? Is she ok?"

"I think so. She's sleeping." I wasn't sure how much I wanted to share.

"And?"

"She tried to hurt herself. "

"Like suicide?"

"I don't know. Maybe. I don't think so."

"How?"

"She used a scissor to cut her wrists."

"Holy shit!"

'Let's keep it quiet, ok?"

"Yeah, sure."

I looked in the paper bag.

"Why would she want to hurt herself?" he asked.

"I don't know. She's sad, I guess."

"Sad? Why would she be sad? I mean… you know what I mean."

"Who knows? I can't figure it out."

His eyes turned down and his body tensed. He wanted to ask a question, but paused before he could speak, like a child who just realized he can't play outside because of the rain and thought it prudent not to ask Mom.

"If you're wondering about the trip, I don't know. I guess we'll see how she's feeling when she wakes up."

"I have these," he said and pulled three small plastic sandwich bags from his pocket, each one contained a small white pill. He handed one to me. "Put it in your pocket for now."

"Everything's in the car and ready to go," he said. "Let me know when you decide. I don't think we'll make the concert at this point, it's like a six-hour drive, but we'll still have fun, right?"

"Yeah, of course. But I really don't know if this is going to happen."

"I know, I know. Do what you need to do, but I hope we still go."

By six o'clock, we were in the car.

6

Lily is having a time of it. I often wonder why we didn't name her after some other charming flower: Rose or Petunia, Blacked-Eyed Susan or Daisy. Lily just sounds so sickeningly sweet, so pure of heart. Yuck. Why not make her sound fearless: Athena or Juno? I had little say in the matter. At the time of her naming, I thought it best to stay out of the way, to be seen and not heard. I've gotten used to the name, just like I was told I would. What about Alexandra? That's the name of a conqueror, someone who doesn't take any shit. Alexandra—stomper of daisies. Focus has become an issue for me of late, another of the wonderfully cruel secrets of the gin drinker.

Anyway, it appears my Lily's marriage has hit a snag. "He's sleeping with his secretary," she informs us in a very un-Lily-like way, then sips her coffee with a squealing slurp and bangs the cup down on the kitchen table to garner the full effect. It's a good way to get my attention.

"Are you sure?" I ask. I can feel Margaret's glare searing into my ruddy, gray-stubbled cheek. Out of the corner of my eye, I can see Margaret biting into her lower lip to the point of bleeding, never a good sign for anyone, particularly me. Forty years on, I'm still the same hopeless embarrassment, the black sheep the family would prefer to quietly tether and gag in the basement during the holiday season to avoid further untidy apologies and explanations.

"Yes," Lily reflects. "At least, I have a feeling."

There it is, my stretch toward that smooth, snow-covered peak of fatherhood we all aspire to climb: being helpful. Now, that my part is over, it's time to lean back into the chair and finish my well-earned, steaming cup of coffee and await the show. No need to cut and run for the hills and prolong the inevitable. I am certain of the subject pivot. My trial is set to begin and one may as well have a prime seat, front and center, for their demise. It's the sporting thing to do. I wait, oddly patient, for the inevitable comparison—*he's just like you*—which, thankfully, and inexplicably, never arrives.

I never cared for her husband, Gary. He has a mocking, deluded sense of self and speaks unceasingly of deals and connections and trajectories without measureable conclusion. He's in the midst of several perpetually evolving agreements that never find time to agree. He's the snappy country club dresser without a club or country, an irritating, thin-lipped sack of wind. "This will change lives," he's said more often than I change my socks. He's full of shit.

His father is worse, Gary Sr., a serial braggart, tall with

perfect salt and pepper hair. He made his money on some impossibly handy invention, like the wheel or right-angle, which, evidently, still pays him monthly residuals. On the thankfully rare occasions when we're blessed with his arrival, it's a tedious, eye-rolling affair that commences with an unmistakable "manufacturer recommended" engine rev of his limited edition, European sports coupe that signals he's both crested the driveway and is nearing puberty. Next is the installation of the emblazoned canvas car cover, a labor of love that requires a series of choreographed steps, folding and unfolding, tucking and pulling, which, twenty minutes on, produces nothing more than an unsightly brownish driveway mound. All the while, his overly manicured companion obediently waits, coat in hand, garish lipstick at the ready. His newest wife is so plied with plastic surgery, she no longer has feeling in her lips, causing her to dribble her drinks down her blouse and onto her newly installed breasts.

"Have you spoken to Gary about this?" Margaret asks. Ah, yes. She's the rock.

"No, I haven't," Lily quips. The shortness of her answer indicates she is looking for a more immediate condemnation of his latest indiscretions.

"Don't you think you should?" Margaret again.

Lily's eyes dart toward me, her head still, neck rigid and lips pursed—I've been found! Apparently hiding in plain sight is a crock perpetuated by a class of innocents, those with little to fear, little weight on their delicate shoulders.

"Dad?"

"I never liked the prick." *Back to not helping.*

Margaret performs one of those *God give me strength* pleads to the heavens, her eyes aimed toward the ceiling and palms up like an Eastern deity, before placing her hands flat on the table. I can only assume her deliberate hand placement, safely in front of her, is an effort to prevent her from flinging a well-earned backhand across my jaw.

"You're not helping," Margaret acknowledges. *I told you.*

But in fact, I am helping. The question is really who am I helping? I'd been provided an opening to speak my mind, to let forth whatever vulgar contempt I'd spent years burying under holiday half-smiles and fishy handshakes. Was it Gary's long-winded stories of importing and exporting of… what? I have no idea; I'd stopped listening. No, it was all of it—the whole shebang—his very person. On more than one occasion that he was in range, his mouth flopping on about something, my hand closed firmly around my rocks glass, swirling the now naked ice cubes, ready to tighten into a fist, shattering the glass and hurling five knuckles toward his pointed red nose and that one hideous stray hair that always juts out of his left nostril. Glorious.

"Tom, don't you think she needs to speak with him?"

"You need to clear the air," I say. "A good relationship, a long term, healthy relationship requires communication and honesty." Where did that come from?

Two heads slowly turn toward me, in precise, stupefied unison, mouths slightly open, eyes pulled into curious, slightly unnerving squints. I wink. What else can I do? I'm swiping a page from Gary's voluminous playbook of bullshit.

I tap the table with the tips of eight fingers and rise from the chair like a chieftain who's provided his final, indispensable council and is off to other pressing matters. I give a tiny, but unmistakable nod to each of them and, without awaiting permission, dismiss myself.

7

The insult rolls off his tongue—"prick"—like he's already started breathing the free air in foolish anticipation that his triumphant council will arrive with news from the parole board. In other words, he took a consequence-free opportunity, akin to a dare, to let fly an honest opinion on a forbidden subject riddled with land mines.

In his usual fashion, Tom skillfully wiggled his way out of a difficult conversation, and tiptoed around the minefield. In many ways, I'm envious. Who else but Tom could simultaneously drop an insult, then, despite all odds, save the day with a steaming dish of dime-store psychology? And this in under a minutes' time. Then summarily dismiss himself, meander through the living room and around the coffee table, pause to stare out the window—all to throw me off the scent—then out to the garage to liberate a half bottle of gin from the drawer labeled "assorted hardware."

"Is he drinking?" Lily asks when Tom was well out of range.

"He is," I say. "No more than usual. Maybe more. I don't know anymore."

Lily goes quiet and gives a melancholy crunch of the nose and forehead and tilts her head, her hair cascading over one shoulder. It's the look we instinctively reserve for funerals, a wordless *sorry for your loss*. Then, "What did you do when Dad was cheating?"

"I wish you didn't have to ask that question."

But Lily does need to ask. She'd been witness to our lives, Tom's and mine, oozing warts surrounding mild triumphs. All the while, my heart beating on the outside—broken, mended, mostly broken again. And here is the result sitting across the table, half-slumped, one hand pushing her hair back over her forehead and—despite her years under the stick of a monstrous ballet teacher, all of ninety pounds and wolverine ferocious—her spine is bent in a nightmarish posture, shoulders thrown forward in surrender. I'm starting to feel bad for myself when it's Lily who needs tending.

"Is Dad going back to work?"

"Bill's called a couple of times, but just to see how he's doing. Your father won't return his calls. I don't think he's ever going back, no. I guess he's retired."

"That's too much free time on his hands," she says.

I shift the topic. "What is it you want from your life with Gary?"

"I don't want your life."

No, I think to myself, *you don't*.

"I'm sorry, Mom," she says. "What I mean is I don't want to live as strangers. You and Dad, you have a small tension that's existed as long as I remember. I don't know what it is, maybe you do, maybe you don't, but it's like a constant buzzing that lives in the background. It doesn't necessarily drive you crazy, but you don't know where it's coming from and when you try to find it, the sound stops. It just exists between the two of you, because of the two of you."

Tension. Yes.

8

Crying.

There was always crying. Unmitigated, soul-crushing sobs devoid of hope and discipline, and without ebb. Before the shock treatments, Susan wouldn't leave her room for days.

Between, I spent hours holding her back from the edge, assuring her she was good enough and pretty enough and smart enough. Yet, each week—almost each day—we started at the beginning, like the prior day's, the prior week's conversation had evaporated into thin air. Progress, in my eyes, was flushed as often as we flushed a toilet, swirling downward toward… somewhere.

I visited her professors and spoke to her classmates to gather assignments, but it was ultimately unsustainable. I do know at some point, I gave up. I stopped trying to make things better and began to hope that they simply wouldn't get worse. Looking back, that's my greatest failure. Forgiving myself has proved elusive.

Now, am I a fool for turning a blind eye even today? Perhaps. Am I a stupid person for forgiving Tom time after time? Maybe. But, like Susan, like myself, and without fault, Tom is broken. And I refuse to hold that against him. It leads to an unforgiveable place. I know that.

There were occasions when Susan turned her vitriol toward me.

"You're not helping! You're not fucking helping!" she screamed. She had a look she would deliver, piercing and so full of hate, it was dryly emotionless, as if the needle of contempt had spun so far around the dial, it was back to naught.

I'd tried to help, to discuss things in what I considered a logical, rational manner. I listened and listened more. I disagreed, softly and respectfully, with doe eyes and a nodding head, when she blamed herself, her beating heart, her wandering mind, her ill-fitting clothes and thick ankles. I stroked her arm with the tips of my fingers all the while attempting to distract her by changing the subject. In other words, I tried to help in a manner that, I assume, would help me when I was distraught or emotionally drained.

It was 5pm. Her hair was plastered against the sides of her head, unwashed and angry in that odd, wire-coiled, 1970's manner that I pray never returns, and her breath reeked of stale cigarettes and broken sleep. There were deep, black arcs beneath her swollen eyes. Her eyelids were outlined in blood red, made worse by the contrast with her damp, pallid skin. Contrary to her rising from the bed that very morning, she looked of death.

First, a freshman psychology textbook, then a transistor radio followed by a glass bowl, goldfish and all, hit the wall as Susan grabbed whatever she could and flung it across the room. The bowl shattered, soaking the floor with reeking swamp water, an algae-covered pink castle complete with miniature fairytale princess (1/1000 scale), and scattering slivers of foot-piercing glass, millions of invisible booby-traps that a thousand cleanings could not fully clear. The castle lay toppled on its side in the middle of the mess, flooded and broken, the princess sheared off at the waist. The fish, a scrawny, orange beast with eyes three sizes too large for its face, didn't struggle long, its attempts to kiss the air in the room, mouth thrown open, did little to satiate its need for oxygen. The fish's name was Hubie or Jeff or something. I think it was Becky's fish.

"You think you are—you think you're so fucking smart! Well, you're not!"

"I need to clean this up," I said.

"Want something to clean up! Do you?" She continued to rage.

"No, I don't," I replied as I searched for a towel to mop up the creeping toxic waste. The odor of the fouled water made me dry heave, turning my stomach inside out and filling my throat with bile.

Susan extended her arm and with one sweeping motion, cleared her desk of any and all contents. Pencils and pens, the ceramic mug that held them, came crashing down and added to the minefield, notebooks and a desk calendar, now soaking in fish shit. Her black desk lamp, caught by the length of cord, was dangling in purgatory, left to contemplate its fate, to await its destiny a few inches from the floor.

"Mags, you have Marsha Brady hair," she said in the odd moment of calm that followed. (Was that a compliment? I'm still not sure.) Then, before I could decide, she followed with, "It's kind of just there, drooping down your face—just blah. You should do something with that, you know, give it some life. I don't know." Her voice and attention trailed off when she grew bored of discussing my hair.

It was in that moment that I turned sour. Unable to find a towel to clean the fish water, I yanked her white tapestry from the wall, and cast it over the floor like a throw rug. It settled onto the wet floor in slow motion.

As I watched my handiwork with arms folded across my chest, Susan lunged at me, digging her fingernails into my face. I could feel the skin separating from my cheek, peeling away from my being, hot, acidic, excruciating. I screamed. She was trying to bore through my face, into my soul, out the furthest end.

As far as helping Susan, it was clear: I failed. Miserably. What pessimist was it that said, "No good deed goes unpunished"? Yes, that was life with Susan. But I would give anything to exist in that life again. We both would, Tom and I.

9

My instinct was to flush the toilet. That is always my first instinct and I dare think most would share the same tendency. Such a simple act, a turn of the wrist—flushing solves so many of life's problems. Drowning the now spent and unwanted before carrying it somewhere else—anywhere else—where, presumably, it becomes someone else's problem. Where does it go, this tepid pool of waste and inert byproducts of life? Such awe-inspiring power we wield in a flush, which, until now, was dutifully performed without a second thought. No protracted trial where seasoned council posit the abstract before forlorn, grey-haired judges, or, for that matter, any consideration before banishment—no parting words, just a murky spiraling downward toward the abyss, never to be seen again. I cared not where it went. Just somewhere else. That is the covenant we hold with modern plumbing and I continue to uphold my end of it. Why this sudden infatuation with such a thing and place?

Sometimes, there are clues in the mundane, small changes in habits, misplaced trinkets, something ever so slightly out of place. Even the most clever among us, the ones who spend their lives deceiving others, can be tripped up while faithfully dotting the I's and crossing the T's. And my Tom does not rank among the most clever.

Just earlier, I'd ambled into the bathroom and switched on the electric light like I'd entered the room for the first time, a statue at the entrance, frozen, eyes tightly in a squint, my hand raised to my forehead to protect them from the light. Not a grand entrance to be sure. My 6am eyes, slowly adjusting to the light, were encrusted in the season's allergies and still blurred with morning fog. When they refused to cooperate, I was forced to balance myself by holding onto the walls as I navigated the room. I felt drunk and dehydrated, off-kilter and slow of thought, though I'd not taken a drink for the better part of a week.

When I'd completed my task and stood up from the vessel, I noticed something odd, shiny and unusual (and surely not of my making) resting in the still waters of the toilet's ivory bottom. I tried a new angle, tilting my head to one side, to see if I could identify the object, moving my head closer, then directly above. It wasn't one of the logical substances one might expect to find in a toilet—in other words, it wasn't related to the traditional digestive process. What a strange moment in time, leering over this cauldron of water, bent at the waist with hands on my hips, intently searching for validation, hovering in the rich gray between confusion and suspicion. Moments passed like hours. Finally, reluctant but without fear, I reached my hand into the yellowed water and fished it out.

It was hard to the touch, thankfully solid. It slipped and slid on the porcelain, resisting the grip of my fingers with a dull clink and scratch. Once liberated, I lifted it toward the light, soiled water rolling off my wrists and down my arms before falling onto the tile. It was a pearl, slightly oval, crimped in discolored metal forged in a different age. I turned it in my fingers, studying it, noting the weight, pinching it to be sure it was solid. The pearl, yearning to be free, slithered from my grasp and dove back into the water. I confidently scooped it out again. There was something familiar about the brownish pearl, old as time and long out of style. We'd met.

I washed it in the sink, hoping soap and warm water would help reveal its secrets; the color refused to brighten despite considerable effort. I dried it with one of the showy towels from the rack, baby blue with embroidered pink and yellow flowers, one typically reserved for entertaining and perpetually off limits. I feared not. How could this pearl have found its way to the toilet's bottom in the master bedroom of my house? Had it slipped away from its unsuspecting owner while seated on the perch, sinking to the bottom and, somehow, remaining unnoticed or was it swallowed, working its way through a digestive system, undoubtedly with painful implications, only come to rest on the bottom of that baleful place? Neither was of particular comfort.

I sat down on the toilet again, rolling the pearl between my fingers, wondering how something of such heft and uniqueness could go missing without being noticed. The tile floor, cold on the pads of my feet, made me shiver, goosebumps burst up the length of my legs then down my arms. Racing thoughts competed with the singing of sparrows outside the window—was their melodious sound a welcome to a beautiful, sundrenched morning, the hope of a day renewed, or an ominous signal the neighbor's murderous tabby was on the prowl? Was the pearl plunked into the water a sober planting of evidence, an intentional act by a man seeking attention from his emotionally detached wife, or confirmation that our curious status quo, a murky blend of love and distrust, remained?

Until this moment I'd admired mornings—the damp breath of optimism, unsoiled and sweetly warm, the sun bursting upward like a sea captain's wife, the unknowing, bankrupt widow, climbing the stairs toward the home's highest peak, hair freshly washed, smiles and foolish anticipation, confident she'll steal a glimpse of her beloved's return to the harbor. All that is ruined for me now, though it was always imaginary. For the foreseeable future, my rising, my first act after casting off the blur of slumber, will conclude with a thorough inspection of the bowl's bottom, a pithy fingering of my own tepid waste, half-expecting a treasure, someone else's treasure, awaits my discovery.

What an oaf I've become. Even when I admired mornings, even yesterday, it was always with starry eyes and dreamy, water colored, *what ifs*? What if Susan were here. What if she'd married Tom and I'd married Liam? Tom would be happy, of that I am sure. Would I? Well, perhaps happier. Such schoolgirl longings and imagination, a slumber party away from filling a blue-lined notebook page with inked balloon-lettered "Tom Loves Margaret" graffiti, hearts and arrows.

But then Susan would be alive, bright green eyes falling upon me, a woman in her sixth decade with lingering, organic sex appeal. Would we have kept in touch? Of course; we were sisters. And Tom was my brother. In truth, Tom and I were better suited to brother and sister. Life gets in the way, of course, raising children, maintaining homes, work and all that. But there would always be time for us, Susan and me. We'd make time for us. All would be right, I believe that.

At least once a month, there'd be a girl's martini lunch at the club—Susan running her long, red nails up the arm of the waiter, giving him a sultry glance, then holding him around the wrist while he stammered like a fool. "Two Club Martinis, dirty ice on the side," she'd say, then a wink and "hurry back," admiring his ass as he walked away.

"He's new," she'd say while approving her manicure. "How old do you think he is?"

"Probably too young," I'd answer.

"Don't be such an old lady!" And we'd laugh.

Susan was always laughing—unless she was crying.

After a few minutes, the waiter would return with our drinks, his straight brown hair falling over his forehead and eyes as he delicately placed the glasses in front of us. He's hurried back.

We would be seated outside on the patio under a yellow

umbrella, overlooking the gardens and fountain. It would be a warm day, June maybe, many of the flowers in bloom and the water around the fountain filled with bright green algae and lily pads. Susan would wear a grand Saratoga hat with white lace and a pink bow, black sunglasses with gold trim, a tight fitting white and pink floral sundress cut low in the front; her legs crossed as she leans back in her chair, her drink raised halfway to her lips. She would own the room. An expectant bride would be touring the grounds, whispering to her doting mother, pointing here and there.

"I asked Katherine if she wanted her wedding here, in the garden. She told me she's her own person and wants something different."

"Different?" I'd ask.

"She said 'I'm not you, Mom.'" Susan would shake her head. "My daughter is such a little bitch," she'd say with a laugh.

"How's my Lily?" she'd ask. "I haven't seen her in months. My goodness, it's been too long."

"Happy," I'd respond. Susan would smile and gaze out over the gardens. Lily was always Aunt Susan's favorite and the feeling, of course, would be mutual.

We'd sip our drinks on this perfect afternoon. Ryan, the afternoon bartender, would be on his game today—I wouldn't request a touch of cinnamon, it'd just happen. I'd breathe in the warmth of the day, the soft breeze carrying fragrances from the garden. We'd have nothing but time.

Inevitably, I'd ask, "And how is Tom?"

"I keep him very happy, as you know," she'd reply, her

eyebrows raised above her sunglasses and her signature smirk. She'd take a sip of her martini, leaving an opaque, red lip print on the glass.

"Yes, I'm sure you do."

A stocky, bald man in a crested blue blazer would stop by our table and take a quick bow. His forehead would be damp and he'd breathe heavily through his nose. "Mrs. Morgan, Mrs. Burns, how are we today?" He'd stare down the front of Susan's dress.

"We're well," Susan would answer, shifting in her chair to allow more cleavage. "But tell me, Mr. Behrens, is our waiter new?"

"Yes, Alan has been with us a few weeks and is an excellent waiter. I hope everything is satisfactory?"

"Apparently, he doesn't know our names or our usual drink order. I find that odd, don't you? I hope he's the only one on your staff who doesn't recognize us."

"Please accept my apologies, I'm sure he will not overlook such important details in the future."

"I'm sure he won't," Susan would agree.

After a few awkward moments Mr. Behrens would say, "Well," eyeing his escape, "please, enjoy your lunch," and amble away.

"Why do you do that to the poor man?" I'd ask, barely able to contain my laughter.

"Sometimes you have to make sure you still can. Fuck sixty!" she'd say as we toast. When she'd raise her glass, I'd see the small pink scars on the pale underside of her wrist.

"Fuck fifty!"

"Fuck forty!"

"Fuck thirty!"

We missed them all. We had no time.

My sad reality is this: Tom was my first choice, but I was not his. There's no escaping it, no sugary tale of love being in front of us all along, no forthcoming fairytale ending. We (our relationship and life) are the collateral damage of Susan's life, beautiful and cut short. We were never meant to be happy, Tom and I, we're what's left after the gruesome amputation, the shards of soul swept up off the floor and placed in a shoebox, given a tube of glue and a slap on the back before being ushered out the door.

Had I chosen Liam during our Cornell weekend (or, more accurately, had he chosen me), had I been the target of his salacious plan, would the world be changed for the better? Not likely, but perhaps I'd still admire the morning and be planning our next martini lunch. But, of course, there'd be no Lily. At least not the Lily we've conceived, our collective flesh, weak and pallid, our shared bad habits and manners. All of it. Has Lily made this all worth it? Of course, yes. And no. What I mean is she is the offspring of imperfection, an imperfect marriage—yes, more imperfect than most. And in our imperfection, have we caused her more damage than one would otherwise endure over the course of a life? I live with latent damage every moment of every day and I fear for Lily. She has no Aunt Susan to swoop in and save the day. Life can have many regrets.

At dinner that evening, I moved the roast to the side and placed the fouled pearl at the center of Tom's plate, providing it with top billing (as it deserved nothing less), propping it up on a spoonful of mashed potatoes to prevent it from rolling off in yet another escape attempt. I placed it several times, removed it and replaced it. Though I struggle to explain why, in the moment, presentation was paramount. If the pearl was not immediately obvious, not shockingly representative of unmitigated treachery, would it fail to conjure the demon of guilt? Would the moment, my clear moment of sanctimony, standing on the high hill, arms folded and eyes cast down upon him, be lost?

First the pearl listed to one side, sliding down, coming to rest off-centered, like a hat two sizes too large. Then it rolled down the makeshift mound, clinking onto the plate and rolling about, staying within reach—a dog fighting the tub to avoid a long overdue scrubbing—yet remaining at arm's length, shivering, head bowed, acknowledging the inevitable. At last, I staged it perfectly, resting it like a Faberge Egg on a royal mount, catching the ambient light with a sparkle, glowing. I double salted the mound as small puffs of steam rose heavenward. If nothing else, I could rest knowing salt would kill him in due time.

Tom arrived for dinner and dropped into his seat with unusual heaviness, a weary traveler finding a long sought bus seat, exhaling weighty thoughts through his nose. If his day had been troublesome or difficult, he'd not shared it with me. Though the threat of snow is months away, he'd spent the afternoon in the garage, fiddling with the snow blower, adjusting this or that, moving levers up and down and tightening random bolts not in need of tightening. A "tune-up" he'd mumbled dismissively, oil and filters. Yes, a "tune-up", I'd mumbled to myself—gin and tonic.

He eyed the unusual garnish—a vanilla swirl lovingly perched atop his favorite carbohydrate, the smoking gun—from the safety of his chair. He turned his head slightly like a confused hound and the color drained from his face, the skin pulled tight across his cheeks save small, but deep, wrinkles in the outer corners of each eye. He neither acknowledged the bait nor ignored it completely, instead eyeing it with a modest curiosity. He picked up his fork in his left hand and studied it, turning it over, then back, like he'd forgotten its intended purpose or how to wield it properly. He played with his lower lip, using his right index finger to flick it, making a wet, almost underwater popping sound—a drowning man perhaps, releasing the last of his air before sinking into the abyss below. He was buying time, stalling, hoping something—anything—would pop into his brain and allow him a means to weasel himself out of this mess. Or better, that I would lob a heavy-handed accusation while jumping up and down on the tabletop like a lurid savage in heat and he could feign the surprise of an innocent, the melodramatic shock of the indignant. Over the years, I've found silence is often a more powerful force than sound.

Before dinner cooled completely, he began to eat around the makeshift pedestal, scratching at the plate with his knife as he cut into the roast, lifting heavy forkfuls to his lips like a condemned man awaiting the walk to oblivion, chewing each mouthful well beyond what was necessary, his trademark grinding of teeth. All the while, I stared at him like an eighth grade girl nursing a crush, watching him eat, definitively recalling how to work a fork and knife, wondering if he'd finally say hello after two years of sitting parallel to me in homeroom. Yes, the schoolgirl analogy again. After several minutes, perhaps wary of swallowing the garnish for a second time, Tom picked the pearl between his thumb and index finger and inspected it closely like he'd pulled a wayward hair from the tip of his tongue, before rolling it into his napkin. He didn't eat his mashed potatoes. There was no mention of it. That was our way.

10

"Let me check the bandages."

'Don't be such a worrywart, they're fine."

The car barreled west down the Mass Pike, tires humming and windows cracked open to allow the cigarette smoke to escape. Liam was driving, left hand casually on the wheel, eyes more on Susan than the road, the seat reclined so far back I thought he might be lying down. Susan was in the front seat bouncing to a new Andy Gibb song on the radio, trying to sing along, laughing when she got the words wrong. The lights of the oncoming traffic were starting to illuminate as the sun set, the pinks and reds created a postcard perfect Berkshire evening.

I'd fallen asleep in the backseat, my face propped up against the cool of the window, knees pulled against my chest for warmth. My head ached. I needed water, but all we had were a few bottles of Pepsi and an unopened case of beer. There were yellow chip crumbs on my lap—evidently

I'd broken into the snacks.

"Looook at that. Thaaaat's a sunset!" Liam said, his words unnecessarily long and drawn out, like he was speaking in slow motion.

"Yeah, whoa," Susan responded.

"Wait! Was that Bigfoot?" Liam said, pointing toward the side of the road.

"Where!" Susan screamed. "No fucking way!"

"Man, you just missed him, he was right there at the side of the road, looking at us. I think he waved."

"Mags! Did you see him! Did you! Can you go back? Go back, Liam!"

Liam's laugh was a nasally snicker like a small child who'd pulled a prank on his sister, but was still hiding in the hall closet waiting for it to spring.

Something was wrong.

Until now, I hadn't noticed the car weaving slightly in and out of our lane, and Liam slowly correcting it in small, leisurely arcs of the steering wheel, only to have the uncooperative beast slide toward the passing lane or the guardrail. It all followed a very orderly pattern, no panicked overreactions that might dump us into the median or send us careening off a bridge, just smooth turns of the wheel, consistent pressure on the pedals.

"Did you take the pills?" I asked.

"Maybe." Liam replied while craning his neck toward the back seat, his right arm stretched along the top of the seats. "Maybe we did, maybe we didn't. I can't remember."

"It's a mystery..." Susan added in a gothic voice, raising

her hands and wiggling her fingers.

"Did you take yours?" he asked.

"No," I replied. I checked my front pocket to make sure I still had it.

"Well, maybe you should."

"We weren't supposed to take it until we got there."

"Teensy change of plan."

"No shit, I know that now."

A car beside us blew its horn and Liam veered back into our lane. The man in the other car was yelling and holding up a fist, maybe a middle finger. I couldn't hear what he was saying.

"Go fuck yourself!" Susan yelled while demonstrating with relevant, thoroughly inappropriate hand gestures and facial expressions. Liam released a wet, snorting laugh. Susan extended her middle finger as the man sped up ahead of us.

A few minutes later, Susan began scratching, first her shoulders, then under her shirt.

"I hate this bra! I hate it. I hate bras and I'm not wearing one anymore!"

Within seconds her bra was over Liam's head, hanging down over his ears. "What big ears you have," she said and laughed.

Liam veered again. This time the car heaved toward the guardrail before he overcompensated and jutted us back into the middle of the highway, the white painted lines running firmly down the center of the headlights.

"Mags, I think you need to drive," he said.

"I don't have a license, I can't drive."

"Sure you can," he said while pulling the car over to the breakdown lane. The clicking of the hazard lights only served to increase my unease.

"I mean, I understand the concept, but I've never actually driven." A flash of heat engulfed my body and I began to sweat.

Susan climbed over from the front and flopped next to me in the backseat, her foot narrowly missing my head. "You can drive," she said, her voice rising, "You can drive like ass!"

Liam slid over to the passenger's side and patted the driver's seat with his left hand. "Come on, you can do it."

After a brief tutorial, and once I stopped hyperventilating, we were on our way. I was driving! It was a horrible, nerve-wracking experience and to this day I haven't fully recovered.

"You can't go forty," Liam said in a tinny voice from what seemed too far away, like I was commandeering a plane after the pilot fell ill and the airport tower was guiding me by radio. "You have to go at least fifty-five."

"I'm trying!" I said. "The window's foggy, why is the window foggy?"

"Alright, alright, I'll fix it. No need to worry."

"You fix that fog," Susan said from the backseat. "You fix that fog, Liam."

Twenty minutes or so later, I pulled into a rest area and parked. My hands were aching and cramped, locked into a ready position at ten and two. Tears ran down my cheeks though I did my best to hide them, mopping them with the sleeves of my sweatshirt. I was done. The drive, however short, had buried me.

"I need to use the bathroom," I said. But when I turned the key into the off position and the engine wound down, I knew this was as far as we were going. We'd crossed the border into New York, but no further.

When I returned from the bathroom, Susan and Liam were drinking warm Narragansetts in the backseat.

"Let me have one of those," I said as I slid into the driver's seat.

Liam looked at me like I'd whistled to a puppy.

"We're not going any further are we?"

"Nope."

A few hours later, I awoke to find Susan, stripped naked, bouncing on Liam's bare lap, their mouths locked, unraveled bandages dangling from her wrists by single strips of white tape. I watched them for a minute, her delicate back glowing in the moonlight, her auburn hair rising and falling along her spine, sweeping side to side, his white, hairless chest, still that of a boy, taking in great innocent puffs of air then releasing them as harried breaths. During a momentary gasp for breath, Liam and I locked eyes, his mouth opened slightly, about to speak, the words refusing to release themselves from his lips. The windows, fogged and translucent, trapped me in the hot oven like some perverted side dish. I found the last mouthful of warm Narragansett in a can buried between my legs and tried to go back to sleep.

It all made sense now. Liam had arranged the entire trip

(all of it, a ruse really) with the sole purpose of achieving this end. His questions were vague enough to evade detection, innocuous enough to defend: how was she? Were we still going? Sure, things happen to tick in his favor: Susan was particularly vulnerable, ready to be manipulated, willing to be plied with drugs and alcohol. Not that she minded. Were there really tickets for a Grateful Dead concert awaiting us in Ithaca? Maybe. More likely our arrival would trigger a small misunderstanding, a miscount of interested people, a last minute change of plan, his brother playing the heel and feigning apology and misunderstanding. Regardless of the reasons given, the harried explanations and excuses, blame would not fall on Liam—he'd be clean. The important thing, the crux of the whole scheme was to get Susan off campus, to take her mind off of her troubles, to unleash Susie in the hopes of… well, exactly this… His plan, as it appeared to me, was masterful.

I, of course, would be responsible for the aftermath, the mopping up—lying to Tom, covering for Liam, reminding Susan that she taken acid—the whole shebang. In the moment, with my eyes squeezed artificially tight, the sounds of their sordid intercourse were amplified from the backseat, including the breathy, histrionic conclusion, the guilty pleasure of release. I was sick to my stomach. I don't think it was pangs of jealousy, a wishing we could swap places and I be the subject of Liam's fancy, which brought on the twisting of my stomach (the soft, but thorough retching), though certainly it's possible. It was what this moment, this dramatic, humid convulsing, represented: the beginning of the end of the four of us. The dalliance, itself, was secondary.

Though we wish them to be, these breakpoints are never clean, no one walking up the gangplank of an ocean liner and with a limp wave goodbye, sailing off to the new world, never to look back, a footnote to history, a memory destined to fade. No, this breakpoint would be an ugly, festering wound, resistant to any attempt to sanitize or explain, to amend the intentions or recolor the actions. There would be no apologies, no insincere attempts at "sorry." Though, as I've described, we embraced all forms of casual touching and vulgar innuendo, free-spirited banter with wide latitude, it was always (for lack of a better term) respectful. Until this moment, it had been fun, good-natured even. There was no place in our insular world for this sloppiness, for deceptions, for greedy acts, the unwritten rules were actually chiseled in stone. We all knew this. I shivered in the seat, the tips of my fingers and the tips of my toes frozen and stiff.

There was also this: I wasn't sure I'd be willing to cover for them, to bury what I'd seen. Liam had to know his grand scheme would shatter our clan, splinter alliances, end things. I was also sure he didn't care if it did, which meant I owed him nothing. I owed her nothing. Of course, my reasoning would require them, either of them, to request my silence.

Susan and Liam threw up with the rising sun. They circled the car like dogs looking for a perfect napping spot on a rug, stomping about in opposite directions before dumping the contents of their stomachs on the rest area pavement, spreading warm, half-digested beer into shallow, yellowish puddles. Liam pissed on the front tire. I offered them tepid bottles of Pepsi as their reward.

I slid over to the passenger's seat to allow Liam to drive. He flopped into the seat, an empty sack of skin, boneless and weary, and slammed the door shut with a smooth swing. He looked at me out of the corner of his eyes and licked his front teeth, gritty and soiled by the night, before reaching for the keys and turning the ignition. The Dodge croaked and huffed before turning over, heaving and trembling before finding its humming groove. Liam pushed his full weight back into the seat and stared forward like his mind was filled with perpetual white noise, the hiss of setting a needle to a scratched record on the turntable. His hair was greased flat against the sides of his head, forming a tall rooster's peak on top. On a normal, carefree morning, it would have been a comical look or even an unintentional homage to the nascent punk rock scene. We would have laughed at his foolish hairstyle or ogled at his perfect ode to anti-establishment. This morning, though, it elicited and searched for an end even before it sought to begin. He'd ended the establishment once and for all.

"Home?" he said without looking at me, his voice weathered and stale, scratchy from the night.

"Where else?"

He rubbed his eyes and, for the second time in the past few hours, turned to me to say something, pulling in a deliberate breath and thrusting his chin toward me. Still nothing. He itched at his crotch, moving around the dried bits of Susan that still clung to him, before shifting the car into reverse, then drive, setting us on our way.

The trip aborted, at least most of the trip, the drive back to campus was dead silent, the car softly bouncing along the Mass Pike. Liam returned his hands to ten and two, staring at the road, almost expressionless save his eyes squinting against the morning sun. We drove east, the Dodge consuming the white lane dashes as I watched and waited, counting each mile marker. Susan was lying in the back seat. In her haste to dress herself, she'd left her jeans undone at the waist and only pulled three quarters up, leaving small, shiny puffs of reddish pubic hair to bask in the daylight. She was clinging somewhere between sleep and nausea, breathing heavily to ward off the hangover demons, burping up small releases of pressure. I rolled down the window of the passenger's seat to clear the uncomfortable stink of sweat and sex and vomit. I checked the front pocket of my jeans, burying my hand up to the wrist. The small white pill was still there, resting safely at the bottom of the plastic bag.

I've never been able to fully forgive them.

11

I wasn't invited to attend the Grateful Dead concert at Cornell, or perhaps I was just busy. Susan and I weren't a thing at that particular moment in time. Or maybe we were. I never knew one moment to the next. It's possible we were "a couple." Our relationship was always subject to her increasingly manic whims: from which side of the bed she'd arisen that very morning, the direction of the prevailing wind, a sad song on the radio—all of these things at once. Our relationship was a constant bend in the road. I could never let my guard down even for a moment for fear of miscalculating the turn and colliding head-on with a tractor trailer barreling down the opposite side of the road. I couldn't loosen my white knuckle grip on the steering wheel for even a moment as the sentinel of trees on my right beckoned my attention, taunted me to veer toward them. It was exciting and horrible and perfect—like Susan.

An optimist would say there was never a dull moment

between us. There was no point where we settled into a bland, predictable nightly dinner and a movie sprawled on the couch under Grandma's crotched blanket, fat and happy, only to emerge on the other end swollen with pent up resentment. There would be no bloated caricature of what could have been, no eventual dressing in the ill-fitting, practical clothes our grandparents wore.

But the truth is, the relationship was a nuclear reactor of stress, a factory with spewing smokestacks and endless conveyor belts conveying things in endless directions, working twenty-four hours a day. And, no matter what had transpired, no matter how insidious the wrong or blatant the transgression, she could find some minute, insignificant detail in which to cling to innocence, or, more accurately, to assign guilt to me. I spent the better part of a year wondering how each and every disagreement, each fight, each clash of personality could be inexplicably viewed as my fault. Really, more than viewed as my fault. I walked away from each altercation, tail between my legs, somehow convinced it was. Of course, we could all own our share, our faults (hidden and otherwise), warts of our consciousness, the inevitable result of simply being conscious. We were selfish and deprived, self-centered, imperfect swine with blinders spawned of needy indulgences and jealousy. But that's exactly the point. We. It took twenty years to decipher how our relationship functioned—twenty years too many.

"Liam fucked me. And I let him."

That's what she said. A declaration of fact, a statement of acknowledgement. No mincing of words, no sinewy justification, no evasive language, no amorphous explanations. Then, she placed the actions of the day on my shoulders, based on my decisions, my behavior, my simmering ignorance.

"If you'd decided to come, it wouldn't have happened. But you didn't want to. Whatever it was you were doing, it was more important than spending the weekend with me."

I was unable to speak. She continued:

"You're the one I love—the only one. Why did you abandon me? Why didn't you want to spend time with me?"

My fault.

And then tears. "You know how men look at me, all of them, all of the time. I don't know why, but they do. They leer at me, they… they sniff the air like dogs. I should never be left alone. They sniff me like fucking dogs!"

I loved her.

There was a commitment to be made—if I was to love her, I had to protect her, mostly from herself.

I've never fully forgiven her, even to this day. Admitting this brings little comfort, but at some point I have to be truthful.

As for Liam and I, things were never the same. How could they be? At the end of the day, he'd hunted her for sport, "sniffed the air like a dog" and knowingly severed the connective tissue that bound the four of us to one another.

Margaret too was complicit, though in a different, perhaps more sinister way. In cutting her wrists, Susan had screamed out for help, let the world know she was vulnerable, unstable, fragile, scared. Yet Margaret ignored the chaos. Instead of seeking help, calling an ambulance or doctor, she delivered my Susan steaming on a Thanksgiving platter, legs conveniently spread, while Liam tied his sordid bib and wrung his greedy hands in anticipation. The pimp and whore worked in perfect, greased unison, all the fixings of a human sacrifice.

And where was I during this ceremony, this orgy, figurative and literal? That's just the thing—I too am complicit in this circle of lust and deceit, though I had the good manners to take things outside of our sacred circle. There is an old saying that I abide by in my imperfect quest: "Don't piss where you sleep." Yes, there was a girl, but one far removed from our daily existence, a long evening shadow, a warm wind rustling the leaves. She was there and not there, on the edge of sight, faceless in the crowd, for several weeks.

Her name was Claret and certainly her hair had blossomed into a scarlet red. An odd moniker, Claret. Perhaps her parents had a penchant for wine, or maybe a blissful sense of humor. I never asked. We met at some smoky, barely lit fraternity party, loud music and nonsense. I don't recall the details, but I do remember squeezing her into some corner of the house, somewhere out of the way, so we could talk. I'd seen her on campus, one of my freshman class great halls where she stood out, at least to me, an apparition of red hair and ivory skin, blue eyes outlined by long, translucent eyelashes.

"Aren't you seeing that girl?" she asked, twirling her finger to indicate curly hair, her head tilted to one side and her nearly invisible eyelashes bouncing—a good sign for me.

"What girl is that?"

"I don't know her name, but I've seen you with her."

"I don't know what you're talking about."

"I'm sure you don't."

"Has anyone ever described you as Claret, Claret?" I smiled to myself—my humor had hit a high water mark.

"I can assure you," she replied, "you're not the first to think they're more charming than they really are."

That night I walked her back to the dorms, stumbled really, though the quad and down the hill toward the athletic fields, her nose cold against my neck as we walked, my hand resting in that perfect concave where her back met her buttocks. She told me about her dog—Lucky? Spot? I don't know—and where she grew-up—some well-heeled town south of Boston that I've long forgotten. We held hands and stopped to kiss on the way, alternating turns stopping and letting our arms extend, jolting the other to a stop before being pulled back toward a warm mouth. We kissed under a towering oak while I held her arms above her head, my hands clamped tightly around her wrists, in the quad while seated on a cold granite bench donated by a rich alumnus whose name was carved in delicate, Romanesque lettering, and on the steps of her dorm, her arms tight around my neck, the outside light flickering yellow and blue on her cheek.

It was a weeks-long affair—if such things deserve that notorious misnomer—a whirl of sex and nothing more. And nothing less. But, considering what you already know about me, my fondness for Susan, what would lead me to this immoral decadence? Why would I wade headlong into these shallow and self-serving acts? What beast drove me when I already spent nearly every night with my love, my perfect match, my person? Good and relevant questions—I applaud you. The answer is the same for all men when confronted with similar lines of inconvenient questioning. The answer does not change whether the man is eighteen or twenty-five or fifty-five or eighty. The answer is simply because she let me. We can skip the heavy-handed psychology lessons, the inquisition, the expense and drone of therapy, the latent damage of misplaced childhood, the grieving, the want and needs of some emotional this or that. Don't waste your time or mine, not another moment of it. I've answered the question.

Though her name was unusual—even unique—no Louise or Jackie, I could not, until recently, recall it. No matter how I tried, there was a void, like her name had been erased to protect the innocent. I could see her face, her hair of course, her eyes. I could even relive her scent, all of her. Unsurprisingly, it came back to me as I sat alone at my desk, considering the facts and options surrounding my Lily's plight, brooding over a vigorous pour of Chianti. Chianti! Claret! If only she'd had the good fortune of being named Tanqueray, her name would never have faded with time, though her parents would have been eyed with suspicion. Susan, of course, would have remembered her name.

It was a Sunday in early June, maybe late May, and I thought there should be more Godly things to be done, though, as usual, I rolled over and ignored them. The tranquil yellow morning held a sky free of clouds. The heat of the sun pushed through the window warming my skin, the bed sheets pulled down low. I'd stayed on campus for the summer, taking a job painting dorm rooms and hallways in what we called "piss" yellow, mowing an occasional campus lawn, that sort of thing. Claret had also stayed for the summer, a kind of guided study with one of the psychology professors, investigating some heady, odd and interesting, yet long disproven theory I wasn't clever enough to fully understand. She'd only just awoken and kissed me gently on the cheek, before rolling out of bed, feet hitting the floor, jolting her as awake as she would be all day. She stood for a moment in the sunlight, naked, her body shiny and damp from sleep and ran her hand over her forehead and through her fiery hair. I studied her curves and breathed her in through my nose, taking it all in, wondering how long it would last.

"Why are you staring at me?" she asked as she slipped on her panties.

"Your body is a work of art—such wonderful lines. I'm appreciating it," I said.

"Oh please! Remember, you're not as charming as you think you are."

"It's a clumsy sort of charming, I'll admit."

"More clumsy than charming."

"But it grows on you."

"It does."

We never said goodbye, Claret and I, or hello for that matter. Instead we had this tribal gesture, this small bob of the head or maybe thrust of the chin that said all that was necessary. That morning was our final head bob, our last chin thrust of the affair. Susan put an end to it—our summer love—put a stop to my dalliances with the "red-headed bitch." She'd let it fester long enough, given me these few weeks, permitted me space to heal, though I never did.

That afternoon, Susan arrived on campus to "patch things up" and get back to it, back to us. But first, before we could move forward, there would be the obligatory reading of the crimes for which I would be summarily executed then pardoned, in that order. It wasn't so much things swelling to a festering boil, this end of semester hand in the cookie jar, but the line of questioning that ensued, the sincerity, the calmness in which Susan took an interest in uncomfortable details. There was no yelling or hopping up and down, no vitriol in her voice. The questions, she had to know, tortured me more than any punishment could achieve. I was sitting on the bed of my dorm room, cowering, praying for a quick reprieve while she prowled the room, back and forth, grinning, like a trial attorney who'd already garnered a guilty plea and was recounting the steps to make sure it was loud enough for the jury to hear.

"Does she have red hair on her pussy?"

"I don't remember."

"You don't remember? How can you not remember? Your mouth was there, maybe even today."

"Ummmm."

"How does she taste?"

"What?"

"Tell me, I wanna know. I'm interested in what you like about it."

"Ok, we're done talking about this."

"Are we? I don't think we are. Show me what you do to her? How she likes it."

"No."

"Is she warm?"

"Warm? What do you mean?"

"Is she warm, inside?"

"I really don't remember."

"How can you not remember? You keep going back for more—why?"

Because she let me.

I could have retaliated that Sunday. It would have been easy enough to press the same foul questions of her and Liam, attempt to make her uncomfortable, to make her guiltily stammer over her words. But I didn't want to know. I never want to know and I certainly didn't want her reliving the experience. And it wouldn't have worked, this clumsy attempt at retribution—she would have made me pay the price for this brazen insolence, a rolled newspaper to the nose. First, she'd ply me with grotesque, haunting details of the tryst, invented or otherwise, followed by that sly, rapturous smile, the aura of her mind being far away in delirious reflection, an allusion to holding back the most scurrilous particulars out of respect for my feelings. No. Forty years later, the thought of their bodies intertwined one evening in May still turns my stomach, spawning dry heaves and bile like someone has pulled my stomach inside out, spilling acid over the rug before running my insides along the honed metal bumps of a cheese grater.

She shifted from interrogator to lover in an instant, without switching hats or tone of voice. She sauntered up to me in the way only she could, all hips and shoulders and a toothy grin—irresistible. My weakness was those lips, thin as they were, the top slipping over the bottom, slightly elongated in the middle, forming a point of delicious, pink flesh. She pressed them to mine, and a cold shiver ran down the small hairs of my neck. I struggled to not kiss her back; I wanted to taste those lips again. As ridiculous as it sounds, those lips gave me the weak-in-the-knees. I loved and feared them more than anything in existence. I wish I had told her.

"Are you going to kiss me back?" she asked with her lips still pressed against my teeth, her arms squeezed tight around my neck.

I didn't respond.

"I've been crying. Alone," she said. "I've been crying for weeks."

I didn't tell her I'd been crying, too, my face buried in a pillow at night hoping no one heard me.

She continued, "Now I'm where I belong."

"I was hiding," I said.

"From what?"

"From you."

"Silly boy," she laughed. "You can't hide from me."

"No, but I had to try."

Had I been there, had I gone on that wretched, aborted trip, none of this would have happened. I suppose we all played our part. Although I dearly wish it could be so, there is no magical genie to grant this request, no humming time machine invented by a lonely, basement-dwelling scientist awaiting my piloting into the past to right the wrongs. The damage cannot be undone. As for that white-bearded fellow with the crook in his back and multitude of clocks at his disposal, Father Time has not kept his end of the bargain. His expected wave of the wand and ancient incantation has fizzled, time passed has not healed me.

I'd see Claret every so often around campus, a head bob in the library or a chin thrust while passing on a walkway, scurrying to class, her unmistakable hair tossing back and forth across her back, her eyes laser focused forward, a faded denim flat cap listing to one side, the apparition in daylight, and that tone of unfinished business. As my father would say, she was a good egg and, unlike me, a forgiving type. When we crossed paths and gave our bob and thrust, she always smiled and winked, played with her hair and said the same thing:

"You know where to find me you're done with that one," she'd say with a dramatic eye roll and disappointed smirk, a shake of head.

But I would never be done and there was no finish, no running of movie credits and sullen music to signal the end of the story. There was no walk, hand in hand, toward the blazing orange of the setting sun. Even long after Susan was dead.

Liam was often sniffing about Claret, strutting like a peacock, scheming no doubt, milling about awaiting her cyclical heat—the burst of pheromones and wanton arousal and blind flail for the closest compatible mate. Or perhaps I'd endured more damage than I'd initially recognized, developed a vulgar paranoia fueled by man's hard-wired drive to compete, this stolid prank of nature upon the males of our species.

Of course, he never looked at me. When we crossed paths, he'd bend at the neck, inspecting his shoes, or rummage through his pockets like he'd misplaced his wallet or lucky rabbit's foot. He always busied himself with something, some innocuous and nervous act, a tightening of his belt or other imaginary thing in need of tending. He wasn't physically fearful of me—no one was—no fair-sighted person shuddered at the rippling display of my double layer of baby fat and narrow bones, and I never threatened him or even threatened to threaten him. Worse for him, I'd just erased him from existence. Going forward, there was a person who, in the past, formed part of our social circle, but he was unnamed and ill-suited for polite conversation, irrelevant. And in the past it was—we were no longer a quartet.

I assume his inability to look me in the eye was derived from well-deserved embarrassment and guilt, a purposeful and reckless foiling of a perfect union. His friendship with three people he'd spend countless hours, days and weeks nurturing evaporated in a self-serving instant. Yet, he continued to chase my tail, to chew on the loose ends, the gristle, and scuttle about in the periphery, a vole tunneling just out of site, maybe to prove his worth to himself, maybe to prove it to everyone else.

This prowling about Claret, wading in the background like a banished specter, may have been his way of garnering my attention, remaining relevant, and ultimately, his hope to win over a pliable, forgiving audience. But there would be no audience, no forgiveness, not from me. In the end, he knew—I knew—his scheming contributed to Susan's death.

Margaret remained friends with Liam for as long as she could and entertained his groveling, I assume. When Susan began to decline, she reassured Liam it had nothing to do with him. She lied. Or maybe she believed it to be true. We've never discussed it. Their friendship was useful to me in that it provided another means of active disassociation, another opportunity to ignore him while plainly in his presence. His greetings and questions to me hung about in the air, puffs of sound searching for an ear, floating, forever unheard. If this all sounds very juvenile and passive-aggressive, something matching a thousand other unpleasant descriptions dripping from the pages of any college psychology textbook, that's because it was. It was deliberate and cruel and I would do so again if given the chance.

12

Things began to unravel further when Susan asked me if I still had the pill.

In September the new semester was underway, but our group was fractured—the milk had spoiled while in the bottle. Susan and Tom were inseparable and no longer talking to Liam. Meanwhile, Liam's desperate attempts to garner Tom's attention were met with a deliberate, spectacular silence. I was left to manage the situation, though had I known what Liam would do next, what he was capable of, I would have also cut him loose.

Susan herself was not better. Her mental state continued to decline though, her outward demeanor remained pure—her game face was intact. Around Tom, she was Susie, gregarious and sexy. When with me alone, she faded quickly, shrinking into a ball of tears, curled under the table.

"Why are you crying?"

"I don't know."

"Did something happen today?"

"No."

"Did Tom do something?"

"No."

"Then I don't understand."

"I can't stop, I don't know."

"Was it Liam? Did he say something to you?"

"No."

"You're not going to try and hurt yourself are you?"

"No."

But she did.

This time, her arms dripping in crimson, I had the good sense to bring her to the campus health center or whatever it was called at the time. I didn't ask her any questions as we walked, her arms hugged tightly across her stomach, shoulders hunched over and stiff. I'd thrown my heather grey sweatshirt over her, the sleeves now stained a dark, brownish-red.

"I'm sorry," she said when she showed me the sleeves. "It's ruined."

"I never liked it anyway," I said and smiled. What else could I say?

She nodded and forced a smile, but her eyes were cloudy and faraway, like she'd boarded an ocean-bound schooner without knowing the destination and wasn't interested in the past or the future, just wanted to be somewhere, any-where else.

When we arrived, she was bundled away by a series of white-coated nurses who looked on with pity and regret, boundless sadness. "Alright, dear," they said.

"Poor girl, beautiful," the desk nurse said, shaking her head as she wrote this or that onto a chart of some sort. "She's all mixed up."

The desk nurse had a shiny face and dark hair pulled back into a tight bun. She was a serious type with fingernails cut down to the skin and powerful, sausage fingers that strangled the delicate pen as she wrote. She was seated behind a pane of glass with two holes, a circular one higher up, presumably to allow the zookeepers to speak to the animals while behind the relative safety of the glass enclosure and a second one, oblong with a flat bottom along the desk for passing papers, pens and maybe for feeding the animals.

"You can sit over there," she said without looking up, pointing in no particular direction.

"Ok."

There were a dozen orange chairs pushed tight against the white walls of the waiting room. None of the chairs were aligned quite the same way, like their nervous occupants spent their time wiggling, trying to escape from the nurse's view. I wandered the room for a few moments, spinning around like a moron, before choosing what I can only say was the least objectionable chair. The stained, rust-orange cushion looked like someone had spilled a bowl of soup onto it, the dried broth formed a cloudy layer of crust, a whitish hue on the surface fabric. Maybe it was puke. Still, it was the least stained of the chairs and was having a far better day than my sweatshirt.

The empty waiting room reeked of rubbing alcohol and

fear and maybe soup, the blue carpet well-worn down the center from the steady pacing of anxious students. I pictured the usual denizens of the room—somber, pallid frat boys with newly leaking genitalia squeezed into this corner and panicked, wide-eyed sorority girls who'd missed their period being reassured by one of their more worldly sisters in that corner. This was not a happy place.

There was some commotion on the other side of the zookeeper's glass, a throwing of hands in the air by one of the nurses followed by, "How should I know?"

The desk nurse gestured a chubby finger to call me over. "She couldn't give us a contact number for her parents. Do you happen to have one?"

"No," I lied.

She gave me a look of exasperation, the frown those in charge dole out when the answers they expect remain elusive, a kind of synchronized eye roll and exhale that confirms our suspicion that they think we're idiots who are wasting their time.

"Can you confirm her information?" She slid a clipboard through the bottom opening of the glass, the paper blue-inked with the basics: name, age, dorm, student id number, etc.

"Looks right," I said and slid it back through. I felt like I'd been fed for the day, my nourishment presented through the opening out of repetition and obligation, but not love.

"She's going to see the other doctor," she said while tapping her index finger on her temple, indicating the doctor for crazy people. Him. The doctor you didn't want to see.

"Ok."

"He's on his way, you can sit and wait if you like."

"Ok." I said. But before I turned toward the waiting room, I said, "I did the right thing, bringing her here?"

The nurse paused for a moment and put down the pen, folding her massive fingers into a double fist on the desk. "Yeah, you did."

In the far corner of the waiting room was a shabby pay phone booth, a wooden antique with a door that folded in half by sliding across, then unfolded for privacy. Unlike Susan's parents' phone number, I knew the pay phone number in Tom's building by heart. I dug a dime out of my purse and closed the folding door behind me. It slammed closed with a clank, creating an air pocket that clogged my ears. I remember feeling like I was in a submarine, I'm not sure why. The boy who answered the phone didn't find Tom, so I asked him to leave a note with the phone number I found in the small white rectangle in the center of the dial and that it was an emergency.

A half-hour later while I chewed off the last of my fingernails, the pay phone rang. I instinctively looked around the waiting room to see if anyone would get up to answer it, but I was the only one there. I took a deep breath before I entered the submarine.

"Hello."

"Mags? It's me. What's going on? Where is this number?"

I attempted to explain the situation in a manner that would not panic him, but that manner, and the skill to negotiate such delicate matters, didn't really exist. I reached for something, some semblance of good news, a roundabout tickle of hopeful imagination, but, no matter, it was futile. She'd cut herself deeper this time, more forcefully and with greater intent. Things, all things, everything, was heading in the wrong direction.

"They patched her up and now she's going to see the other doctor."

"What doctor?"

"Someone who deals with this sort of thing."

"Like a psychiatrist?"

"I guess. They didn't say."

"I'm sick to my stomach. They're going to send her home."

"We don't know that."

"I'm coming down there."

"No, Tom, please don't. She'll be so embarrassed. You can't. It will make it worse."

"How can I not be there?"

"Trust me, she's been through enough already today. Stay there, I'll call you when I know more, ok?"

There was a pause on the line, sadness, wind whistling through the broken windows of an abandoned house, rustling the cold sheets of a long empty bed. His voice grew higher than normal and softer, another soul, arms fully extended, powerless but pushing anyway, trying to save the failing levee from the rising floodwaters. "Why would she hurt herself?"

"I don't know. I'll call you."

"Promise?"

"Yes, of course."

"Say it."

"I promise."

I hung up the phone before he could ask more questions.

The desk nurse was eyeing me from the other side of the glass, one eye almost closed like a pirate, tapping an exhausted pen against the desk. Hadn't she seen the zoo animals in panic before, the look of pure terror, ready to stampede out of desperation? I tried to ignore her and sat back in the soup chair, pulled my knees up to my chest and leaned my forehead on my kneecaps. For a moment, I caught an odd scent of chicken broth and celery, maybe diced carrots. I may have fallen asleep. I was in my mother's kitchen wearing her red and white checkerboard apron, the baking apron I gave her on Mother's Day when I was ten, doing… something. I'm not sure exactly what it was I was cooking or baking or intending to cook or bake, but it made me happy. I dreamed it was last year or even yesterday or ten years from now when everything was simpler. Before, or much after, the troubles.

"Excuse me! Excuse me! Hello!"

It was sausage fingers, this time wagging her tongue as well as those stumpy, chewed down and morose digits. What a brute! The curt manner of the beast, the indelicacy of her demeanor, the voice—acrid and tinny like a crow entering its final season—drained my patience. If this was a place of healing, shouldn't it be at least somewhat comforting or was that only possible in dreams?

"Can you come here a minute?"

I wiped the sleep from my eyes with my wrist, my body felt heavy and unwilling, requiring more energy than I possessed. When I reached the desk—face against the glass—I noticed the rings wrapped around one of those fingers, a wedding band and engagement ring, both three sizes too small, grotesquely strangling the life from that finger, squeezing it into a swollen, hourglass shape. The skin on the finger had a slightly bluish color or was at least less pink than the other ones on her hand and the very tip was paste white. I hated her a little less now.

"She'd like you to join her in the doctor's office."

"Me?"

"You are Margaret?"

"Yes."

"Follow me, please."

I followed her down a narrow hallway that meandered forever, corner after corner of never-ending, brown commercial carpet. I was surprised by how small and insignificant the building looked from the outside, but how vast it seemed now. Being on the inside of the asylum had altered my perspective.

Did I say asylum"? I didn't mean that in the literal sense. We were at a college health center, nothing more. I use the term more to illustrate the leap we'd taken, mostly Susan, of course, but all of us. We were seeing things from the other side now; we were part of it, in deep, up to our eyeballs, accomplices. From this point on, actions were our actions, responsibility was our responsibility, tragedy was our tragedy. It was no longer simply a friendship, it was a covenant.

The desk nurse knocked on a heavy brown door just below the metal placard, Dr. So-and-So—I can't remember his name. There must have been a response and the nurse opened the door and stepped aside to allow me to enter. Dr. So-and-So was sitting at his oversized, dark wood desk, leaning back heavily into his black leather chair while Susan sat on the other side next to an empty, expectant chair. They were smoking and a thick cloud of exhaled fog hung between the desk and the ceiling. I heard the popping of Susan's lips before she sent a stream of blue smoke into the air, a semblance of normalcy.

"Come in, you must be Margaret. I'm Dr. So-and-So. Have a seat, please."

The door closed behind me. I looked over my shoulder when I heard the door latch, then stood silently with my hands at my side, back to the door, neither fully in nor out of the room. The odor of exotic cigarettes and dad cologne hung in the air. Susan gave me a small nod to let me know everything was fine, that, at the moment, she was fine too. I clumsily shuffled across the room, nearly tripping on my own feet, and sat next to her. The chair was far more comfortable and, thankfully, less stained then its counterpart in the waiting room—maybe this was where the healing was supposed to begin.

Susan showed me her bandaged arms, raising them in the air like she'd won a stuffed bear from some pimple-faced game attendant after knocking down a pyramid of milk jugs at the county fair.

"Stitches this time! Fuck, yeah!" she said with a celebratory shriek. Susie had arrived.

"Yes, lovely," I replied, my arms crossed tightly in front of me.

"Cigarette?" the doctor asked. "I have them shipped in from the Canary Islands."

"No, thank you."

"So, Margaret, first, thank you for taking care of Susan and bringing her here. She's doing much better as you can see. You did the right thing."

"Ok."

It didn't take ten years of medical school and mediocre grades on the medical boards to sense my discomfort.

"No need to be nervous, this is a safe place for everyone. Everything we discuss is between us. Susan wanted to bring you in to hear our options moving forward, our plan, I guess you could say. Susan would rather her parents not know about this incident and about our treatment plan, which is fine, totally her decision, but wanted you involved. Is that ok with you?"

"Yes."

"Ok, great," he said and folded his hands in front of him.

He was a stout, desperate-looking man with rolling, bushy eyebrows that were plucked clean in the center at the bridge of his thin nose. The framed, gold-embossed degrees and certificates hanging on the wall behind him told me he was both ranked first in his class and likely the last to lose his virginity. The light from the desk lamp reflected off his greasy, hairless head like a second sun while my own oily image stared back at me, blinking, distorted in time like a carnival mirror.

My next impression of the doctor was more worrisome. As he sat behind this monstrous desk, attempting, but failing, to retain an air of professionalism, he looked at Susan not as a healer, or what I would expect of a doctor, but, first and foremost, as a man. He too carried that lustful, mouth open gaze fawning men settled upon when in her presence. She'd removed the bulky sweatshirt during her earlier treatment, leaving behind one of her flowered, hippie shirts in light cotton fabric, shoulders exposed and loose around the arms, tight in the right places. His eyes were focused on her, examining the right places, imagining whatever sordidness men imagined in her presence. At that moment I knew, at some point, he would try to sleep with Susan. And he held all the power.

"So what we want to avoid is this incident being applied to your record, your school transcript. That makes things… messy. We don't want a label, see?" His eyes now darted back and forth between us—I was there to be the rock, the voice of reason, the trusted confidant.

Susan nodded along as he spoke and looked toward me with raised eyebrows, indicating this part of the speech was for my benefit, prepared and edited to garner my support. The doctor's wet breath made its way across the desk, steaming the glossed surface as it spread in shallow waves. I sat back deeper into the chair, further away from the desk, and crossed my arms again.

He continued, "We also don't want to send you home, correct?"

"'I don't want to go home," Susan confirmed, a newly lit cigarette popping from her lips. "Definitely, not that."

"Right, or someplace, well, to a facility of some sort."

"No, I definitely don't want that either."

"Right, so we have an option, to avoid all that, but I need you to agree to participate."

"Yeah," she replied. "Let's go, man. Let's do it. Count me in."

This is painful to admit, but there was a moment, more than a moment, when I thought: if Susan goes home, if she were gone, I'd have Tom to myself. Yes, in that moment, with Susan's cuts still fresh, still leaking life and her, not long removed from the precipice of death itself and only now receiving the help she desperately needed, I focused on the selfish, the raw deceit of our friendship. Yes, the trusted confidant. If I could conjure this evil while my best friend suffered not two feet from me, while she'd endured her demons in sweat-soaked convulsions, what was I capable of doing? Me, in my high neck white knit sweater and straight hair and bangs cut with no particular style, competing with her, all sex appeal and personality. I always knew I would lose, just the form my loss would ultimately take, the amorphous steadily hardening into the concrete, was unexpected. Only now, softly cradled in this loss, our loss, is the miracle of the concrete, my Lily. Lily does not exist but for the loss of Susan.

Could it be one of nature's ways of achieving balance? For example, in my assessment, larger people tend to have an advantage in youth, the time for sports and war, potential mates thrown over a meaty shoulder and carried off, while small people gain the advantage as the years roll on, fewer resources consumed, less aching wear and tear on the bones, less disease of the heart, a longer life. Perhaps it also works with the attractive and the average-looking. The attractive among us have the advantage in youth, easier on the eyes, subject to the rapturous intoxication of mating, while those of us with average appeal often fade into the blurry background, reluctantly waiting our turn, our long-awaited redemption as vessels of procreation. The average tend to hit their speed bumps and disappointments early on, frequently smoothing out in middle-age, our expectations held in check, our acceptance as our superpower, while the attractive spend their latter mornings in a state of disbelief, desperately searching the mirror for answers tucked deep into wrinkled and discolored skin. These are neither the results of scientific study nor the accounts of experts, just the observations of an average in search of justification.

Was there no one else in the world at the moment? Did no one exist other than me? How sad and selfish this appalling existence, both current and future. And how prophetic a thought. There are things for which you can never forgive yourself, those mucky, sad decisions and actions (yes, even thoughts) that churn your tired stomach each morning long before your feet hit the cold, unforgiving floor. I've spent forty years working through my moments, an ever festering growth and I haven't reached a point where I can put it to bed, where it can rest even for a day. No, I can't justify my thoughts. And, bigger picture, there is little happiness in our world. We're two broken souls, Tom and I, wandering untethered through time, attempting to hold each other together as best we can. That is our only goal, holding together, especially for Lily, until our end itself, until that end comes.

"What do you think, Maggie?" Susan asked.

I hadn't been listening. All I'd seen was the doctor's mealy mouth bouncing about, spewing dusty platitudes while his eyes undressed her.

"If you're comfortable with what the doctor suggests, then I'm comfortable with it," I said without comfort.

"This will be three times a week for the first few weeks, then we can work our way down to once a week," the doctor added. He gave a comical shrug and laughed like he'd asked a question where he already knew the answer, like a sinister plan was coming together at the conference table on the second floor of a still secret, evil lair.

"Yeah, ok," Susan agreed.

Nurse Fingers set up an appointment for Susan for the following week while watching us out of the corner of her eye, trying to figure out if we were together, more than friends, one of those modern college-girl relationships she'd read about in the tabloids.

On the walk back to the dorm, I asked Susan about the appointment, an effort to fill-in the gaps created by my daydreaming.

"I could tell you weren't listening," she said and smiled. She didn't seem to mind. "He said lots of words."

"Sorry, I just kept thinking he's creepy. I didn't like the way he looked at you. Kinda gross."

"Oh, he's a creep! Those eyebrows! It's like he's part grizzly bear." She paused. "I just want to be better. I don't know. Maybe his treatment will work. He's confident it will. "

"What treatment specifically?"

"Shock treatment. I'm going to be a science fiction experiment. Cooked like a chicken with electric shit sticking out of me. A roasted mess!"

She delighted in that phrase, "a science fiction experiment," almost tragically endearing. She referred to it on several future occasions, rolling it from her lips like an optimistic birdsong of spring while her flailing hands, fingers extended, indicated future pain, but a sparkling hope for the day that only she could fully appreciate. Even in suffering she found joy, perhaps nature's final gift to the attractive.

13

Breakpoints in life are uncomfortable. Water is wet.

I've often wondered, when would come the day, the final day when I was too old to chase girls and too decrepit to enjoy the sweet metallic song of gin. When would be the day when the girls would no longer let me, when I was no longer desired and the weight of my liver caved in upon itself. Would I fade off into oblivion? Would that be the day I focus my remaining time and energy, if any, on Lily and Margaret? As you've learned, I'm a shallow man, an unredeemable slouch, one to be avoided, perhaps even shunned and persecuted, dragged into the square and stripped bare then lashed bloody before an excitedly giggling crowd. Excuses? Well, yes, I have them—cowardly and narcissistic, I care only for myself. But, there is a twisted logic, or perhaps just another excuse: it prevents being hurt again, being sent through the butcher's grinder like scrap cuts of beef saddled with fat and gristle, and coming out on the other end, transformed, mashed, blended, twisted.

I have too much time on my hands.

One obvious conclusion is I continually try to replace Susan—a crawling on my knees search of the infinite haystack for the bloodied needle, to find that which was lost, to capture a perfect moment then repeat ad infinitum. Don't we all? But that is too simplistic, too easy, overly trite. The other piece, hidden and also irreplaceable, is I yearn to replace the lost *me*. The me who found the girl, fell in love and lived happily ever after. The me who understood the bird in hand, how rare and wonderful it was, and was blessed with the rose-colored ability to embrace heaving warts as beauty. Ah, poor fool me, neither will be replaced or duplicated, nothing will. Life does not work in smooth transitions or provide fools second chances at that which is lost or abandoned, despite hope beyond hope. And that I find is the saddest thing of all.

I have too much time on my hands.

Why do I drink? That is a question. I'm not sure why anyone drinks. Why would they subject themselves to such things bad for the health, bad for relationships, bad for careers, bad for breath, bad for life? It seems most people drink to be social, to lighten the mood, to be able to interact with lowered barriers, without fault, without anxiety of who they in fact might be. Some people drink to hide, maybe to be someone else, maybe to dull the pain or whatever it is they might be feeling at the moment. This is all conjecture; of course, I have no idea what haunts the dreams and waking hours of others. And I have little care. But for me it's different. I decided long ago it wasn't to hide and it certainly wasn't to dull the pain. Instead, it's to feel the pain, to experience the next morning's tightening of capillaries and throbbing of the head, to punish myself, to relive days past. I'm too much the coward to dare hurt myself by other, more overt and effective means, so instead I spend my mornings in tortured bliss, nature's crooked thumb and nail pressing on my brain, a waterless tension that strangles pain into the head, in the liver and hopefully shortens my life. I imagine my brain being strafed with artillery fire launched from camouflaged gin bottles concealed in hillsides and hammocks of oak and maple trees. My brain is pocked with impact craters and littered with shrapnel buried three inches deep, before being pulverized to dust, ready to be swept into a neat pile with a straw witch's broom and tossed into the wastebasket or used to stoke fading embers in a fireplace. In the end, as always, a physical throb in the brain is more tolerable than the incendiary bomb of memory. I have too much time on my hands.

The drinking grew worse over the past few years, though I overheard Lily claim she didn't think it was possible it could get worse. My Lily is also a fool, like me, though I think the world of her. She fancied herself a romantic too, but was taken in by a scoundrel. This Gary, her Gary, is too much like me and while I understand him—because I understand him—I hate him for it. But, the thing about scoundrels is, as much as you may hate them, may want to lash out with pointed examples of their scoundrel-ness, there is no greater critic than themselves. They come across as confident and happy, but they are missing something inside; there's a void they mistakenly believe they can fill. There's a special place in Hell for scoundrels and that place is among the living.

It's possible my drinking would have increased over time as a result of alcohol tolerance or merely boredom or an unfortunate habit burrowing deeper into daily life. I'm sure my arrival at this level of self-abuse was destined, written in ink in a human skin-bound ledger shelved in Lucifer's accounting office. But, just to make sure, I hurried it along.

I spent most of my life as a consultant, fittingly, a professional scoundrel, who told people when to cut jobs and how to save money, to be that outside voice prompting them to do something they wanted to do anyway, but needed a place to transfer the guilt and point the finger. I made some people rich and others poor, and along the way did well for my family. The travel, no doubt, provided a beard for my vices, crossing oceans, over mountains, across bridges and through tunnels. For the weak, escape will ultimately prove their undoing.

As I mentioned, no one hates a scoundrel more than the scoundrel hates himself, sneaking up on a morning mirror to peek at the lines settled in the corner of his eyes, each day a little deeper and more clearly defined, the heavy circles beneath, dark and discolored, blue, black, sometimes gray. The morning mirror does not lie. The scoundrel lives in a land of perpetual disappointment and gnawing guilt, a land without frontiers or borders, an infinite realm with infinite possibilities, all of which end on a foggy morning standing in front of that honest reflection. The more sinister, invisible lines and wrinkles imprinted on the mind are my only fear in life. My appearance is secondary.

One foggy autumn morning, Sandra flew to Nashville to meet me. Census Bureau business, she claimed to all who inquired, though I'd boldly arranged the flight through my office and on the company dime. Sheer arrogance and blatant disregard for whatever civility holds together a society—that's where I stood at the particular moment in time. In the company rented hotel room, after a company expensed meal, in the company rented car, yes and yes. Seldom is one life destroyed alone—there's always collateral damage, always more than meets the eye. There is no hiding, only denial.

Her suspicious husband, the aforementioned Mr. Hooper, had begun digging around, making phone calls and asking pointed questions with pointed fingers. He'd already rung Margaret to ask, slyly and under the guise of procuring his favorite barbecue sauce, if I was traveling to Nashville anytime soon. And yes. Perhaps Mr. Hooper—wrinkled forehead and weak chin—possessed more street smarts then I'd given credit. Either way, my insular world was shrinking, and the owner of the antique pearl had wandered into the garden and was soon ensnared in the same choking wire trap. We, Sandra and I, were oblivious to the amateur sleuthing, and went about our rakish business, our carrying on, without hesitation, never peering over our shoulders or peeking above oversized and opened menus to scan the room for moles. There's an underappreciated comfort in brazen acts, a natural defense in acting, well, natural. Nothing attracts more unwanted attention than the paranoid thief hiking up a shirtsleeve before turning his wrist to check the time, loathsomely staring down each passerby, lifting the tablecloth expecting to glimpse a spy kneeling beneath the restaurant table, tape recorder and camera at the ready. The brazen are more inclined to enjoy the moment. They deal with the consequences when they arise rather than being tortured from the get-go. The paranoid thief should stay in bed, enjoy the warmth and comfort of wool blankets (forest-green and stained with remnants of homemade chicken soup and mother's love), the softness of the sheets against their bare bottom, instead of turning to the harshness of the dark professions. It's simply not worth it. These fellows are not cut out for this business though they are often blissfully unaware until it's too late.

The sound is scorched into my mind, shattered glass and twisted metal, searing rubber and asphalt. And the smell, sometimes I still smell it when I wake from a sound sleep: burnt rubber and blood, dampness, salty piss wet on my pants. And also Sandra's wonderful, flower-hinted perfume floating softly in the air, the scent kissing me awake, caressing my nose. Yet, I don't remember much more. Did I turn into oncoming traffic on purpose?

What if things were different—all of it? What if I'd married Susan and Margaret had married Liam? Would I be happy? Would Margaret?

I see Susan on a summer afternoon, seated at an umbrella-shaded lunch table, leaning back deeply into the chair with one bared-leg crossed over the other, the slit of her yellow sundress teasingly riding up her thighs. The diamond necklace I gave her for our twenty-fifth anniversary rests softly on her tanned skin, delicately sparkling whenever she turns her neck. She moves a long strand of auburn curl away from her face and tucks it behind an ear. Her perfect lips are glossed cherry-pink and slightly open; she's looking across the table at me like she's decided I'd make a suitable mate.

Yes, he'll do just fine, she's thinking.

The consummate jackass, I'm focused on the small lines, the wrinkles tucked into each side of her mouth.

"Those lines are from smoking," I tease, ever the smooth talker who knows just what to say.

She laughs at me because I'm too foolish to know better. I attempt to recover by reminding her she's still the sexiest woman I've ever met. She doesn't hear me.

"Smoking's been out of style for years. I haven't smoked since the seventies," she reminds me with a laugh, pointing both index fingers toward the corners of her mouth. "These are frown lines brought on by my dear husband."

"He's not so bad, is he?" I ask sheepishly.

"No, he's not so bad. Smooth talker, that one."

I stare at her, gawking, breathing every ounce of her in, her presence, the way she looks back at me over the rim of the glass before slowly taking a drink from her martini. She still owns the room after all these years and it's not even close.

"What are you staring at?" she asks, her cherry-pink lips puckered.

"You." She knows, of course.

"You mean the ugly lines on my face?" She smiles and rests her chin on her palm, elbow planted on the table, and raises her eyebrows awaiting my next gaffe, my next predictable fumble.

"No, just you."

She allows me the moment.

"I'm having lunch with Margaret tomorrow."

"How is Mags?" I ask

"Good. Seems happy, doesn't she always?" she says, her voice pitched higher to accentuate the perfection of Margaret's existence, singing like a sparrow in a daisy-covered field.

"Still married to Assface?"

"Thirty years."

She shakes her head slowly and frowns at me, deepening the lines at the corners of her mouth—my frown lines, I've earned them tenfold—then summons that faux parental scolding face and slow, methodical voice women reserve for naughty children and hopelessly brutish husbands. "He's been good to her for all these years, you could at least use his name."

"I thought I did."

She smiles and shakes her head again—I'm impossible and immature, just the way she likes me. And I've never been happier.

"Ah, such maturity, I'm so proud of you," she says.

"You've come so far in only forty years."

"Thank you," I reply and take a drink from my glass of ice water.

The waiter, a surly fellow with thin lips and a greasy comb-over that forms a peak in the middle of his head, ambles over and asks me if I'd like a "real" drink.

"I don't touch the stuff," I tell him.

"Don't mind him," Susan replies to the waiter. He's assumed that petulant and slightly exasperated waiter pose, eyebrows pulled upward and pen raised at the ready. "He used to be fun."

"Don't listen to her," I attempt to defend myself with a wave of my hand. "I was never any fun."

The waiter is not nearly as amused as Susan and I. He forces a half-smile and exhales loudly, a sort of compulsory laugh, a middling attempt to satisfy the establishment's written service guidelines, and waddles away into oblivion.

"Has Scarlet decided on grad school?" I ask. "No surprise, she hasn't called me back." The father is always the last to know.

"No, she's going back and forth. Indecisive, like her mother."

"And a little bitchy, too," I add with a smile.

"You wouldn't have it any other way," she says, her tongue resting on her top lip, her eyes squeezed into slits.

Not for the world.

The sirens, piercing sounds and flashing lights—blue, red, orange—people in powder blue shirts and pinned on badges moving about in a frenetic blur of activity. My head thick with sounds, dizzily stuffed full, like it was being pumped up with air until there was no room for more, though it kept arriving from every angle. I was breathing through my mouth, slung wide open, the harsh, acidic aroma of percolating oils and fluids escaping their captivity, spilling forth like school children granted an unscheduled recess, burned my throat. There was a man at the window, or where the window used to be, one of those powder blue types with serious blue eyes pitted too close together and a thin nose curved upward at the tip.

"Sir, can you hear me?"

"What?"

"Can you hear me?"

"Yes."

"What's your name?"

"Tom."

"Tom, I'm Wayne. Do you know where you are?"

"No."

I was staring at my hands, thinning skin and brown age freckles covered with blood, flipping them from back to palm. I didn't know where the red was coming from, what was leaking out and from where. A breath of Sandra's perfume poked me on the temple; I turned my head toward her. The car was caved in upon her, the hammer, the brunt of the impact fell upon her door. She lay crumpled, broken beneath metal and glass. Her presence was fading. There was no sound. I could no longer smell her perfume. All I saw was red.

Another car came to rest a few feet away, the hammer itself, the front smashed inward like a discarded accordion. I could see someone in the driver's seat behind a spider-webbed windshield, flashes of gesturing hands and a purposeful shaking of a head. There was another powder blue type at the driver's window confidently nodding and pointing like he was the architect of this particular stretch of road and knew every square foot by heart. People were milling about, some hurrying back and forth, others unsure where they should be, standing alone, trying not to make eye contact.

"Tom, can you wiggle your fingers?" It was the thin nosed man again, Wayne, leaning toward me, his gloved hand on my shoulder. I thought he'd gone. "What's her name?"

"Sandra. Is she ok?"

"Tom, we're going to need to get you out first so we can help Sandra."

"Did I piss myself? I think I pissed myself."

Wayne ignored me.

"Can you move your arms? Show me. Ok, good. And your legs? Ok, good."

14

Susan insisted I accompany her for her first treatment with Dr. So-and-So. She wasn't as nervous as I expected, not as nervous as I would have been in her shoes. In fact, she was downright chatty.

"I just want to be better," she said as we walked the brick pathway. "Whatever that may be. I'm not even sure what that looks like."

"They used to torture mental patients with this stuff," I said.

"Perhaps I need a little torture in my life," she said and laughed. "You know, something kinky."

"You're sick," I said.

"See, I told you," she replied and laughed again. "Oh, and I was going to tell you, Tom had bacon and eggs this morning."

Was she was trying to move toward lighter conversation, something to take her mind off things?

"I wasn't with him at breakfast," she added. "You know how I know what he ate."

It took me a moment. "Oh, gross!"

While in the waiting room, I avoided eye contact with Nurse Fingers as she wallowed about her glassed pen, shuffling papers here and there, playing a protracted game of hunt and peck on the clanking, antique typewriter. Every now and then she'd look up at me and release a heavy, rehearsed sigh, like she was hoping I'd abandoned her waiting room the next time she looked up and was continually disappointed. I, of course, smiled back and wiggled my rear-end into my special chair just a little further, wringing out as much comfort as it could possibly provide. We played this little game for the better part of an hour, pausing only when I attempted to use the restroom only to find it locked tight. I had no choice but to ask her for the key.

"Why do you need it?" Nurse Fingers asked with her patented brand of indignation and tough love, a sort of Catholic school nun meets grizzled railway drifter.

"What?"

"Why do you need the key?"

"So I can open the door."

"Why do you need to go into the bathroom? So you can smoke?"

"So I can pee," I said with a special emphasis and elongation of the last word.

Though she appeared unsatisfied with my answer, lips curled upward like she smelled something unholy, she slid the key, attached by a chain to a foot-long hunk of wood, through the hole in the glass. The wood anchor was surprisingly dense and heavy considering it had looked like a No. 2 Ticonderoga in her meaty hands.

"Make sure you return it," she sneered.

"Well, maybe," I said as I snatched it from the counter. "It would just look so good with the other keys in my private bathroom key collection."

The No. 2 Ticonderoga made a lovely thumping sound when I returned it, bouncing off the desk before a greedy hand seized it and dragged it back into the fishbowl like an incarcerated man reaching through the bars of his cell for a daily meal. I reflect back on this seemingly innocuous moment of rebellion not for the act itself—I was purposely being an ass—but as a fleeting moment of power in a futile struggle, a brief moment of clarity considering all the while we were being bamboozled.

I know it was my imagination, but I swear I could smell burning wires, or worse, seared flesh, wafting into the air of the waiting room, suspended over me as I sniffed, floating like a fat cartoon man following the scent of an apple pie cooling on a windowsill. I may even have heard a hiss, a sizzle or caught the pop of a spark shooting skyward from the torture device. The dials and gauges sprung to life in electric euphoria, the white-coated and wire-haired mad scientist cackling and running about the room. I'd seen too many movies.

Susan emerged in a state of contemplative confusion, like she was solving complex equations in her head, calculating this and that and hadn't the time to acknowledge me. She walked straight into a wall, more of a glance, but enough to bring her back.

"Hey," she said from somewhere dreamy and far away.

"You ok?" I asked.

"Ummm…yeah. Well, yeah, sure."

"Do you need to sit down?"

"No, no, I'm… good."

"How was it?"

"It hurt a bit. It's supposed to induce a seizure, so it hurt."

"A seizure?"

"Yeah, a fucking seizure."

"That's a scary thought."

"Next time he's going to give me a pill to help the pain."

"What kind of pill?"

"I don't really remember. It was all like a dream… like being born on a foggy morning."

We walked back to the dorm in silence, the light scraping of our shoes on the brick our only company. For some reason, I remember her walk that day, even in her slightly delirious state—she carried herself better than I could on my best day. How can I describe her walk? Elegant and smooth, sultry, her legs carrying her without effort, her body in perfect synchronization, shoulders pulled back, all pivoting and sliding on polished and lubricated muscles and joints. Her pace, as usual, was very fast, like she was supposed to already be somewhere, but the movements moderated the appearance of haste, like she was running in slow motion. She walked like nature wanted you to follow her. I put her in my bed for a nap and she slept the deep sleep of the dead.

Tom collected her that evening and thanked me for being such a good friend, her best friend. He confided to me his biggest fear was not being mentally equipped for Susan's journey, as he called it. I told him none of us were equipped for it, but we'd learn, we'd adjust along the way. What choice did we have?

It was also the first time he told me he loved me, really told me, his warm breath whispering it into my ear as he hugged me. Though I did not doubt his heart, I knew his love for me was different than his love for her. I reluctantly accepted his gratitude despite my conflicted thoughts, the trembling and secret desire to usurp her. Yet, I loved her. I didn't want to knock Aphrodite from her glorious perch, I didn't want harm to come to her—I wanted to be her. I cried that night; I'm sure we all did.

That was the only time I accompanied her to an appointment with Dr.—I have to think of his name—Inslee. I think that's the name Patrick used and it sounds right. She received treatment three times a week for several weeks, then once a week for a few months. Each treatment began with doses of muscle relaxants and some kind of narcotic that was supposed to dull any pain. Nurse Fingers scheduled the procedures around Susan's classes so she could sleep for several hours after. As I would later learn, the treatment when combined with these drugs was experimental, a pet project of Dr. Inslee and hardly accepted practice.

Other than complaining of fatigue, Susan didn't offer much feedback on the treatment. She didn't really discuss it at all. Instead, when pressed about her mood and how she was feeling, which I'm sure became burdensome rather quickly, she pushed on us, her audience, asking what we noticed in her behavior.

In truth, I noticed very little, which (upon reflection) was exactly the hope. She was Susan and Susie and Sue, sans much of the manic shifts and self-injurious behavior. There were moments, to be sure—we all have them—but the road had smoothed out, the ruts ground down and the potholes filled with gravel and tarred over. For several months, all was quiet and normal. Until it wasn't.

15

"Happy?" Hooper asked, his thin lips pulled tight across his face. "Are you happy now?"

"About what?" I asked in a cloud of pain medication, my mind floating high above the hospital bed, scratching against the rough plaster of the ceiling. No, I'm standing, in this threadbare hospital gown, the glowing skin of my bottom proudly on display. There are horses drinking from a mountain river and trout or salmon frolicking, piercing the surface before crashing back into the icy water. The water, gurgling with the melt of snow, sweeps over my feet, then my ankles, then my knees, rising. Rising.

"You almost killed my wife!"

"Margaret is here?" I asked.

"What? I'm not talking about your wife, I'm talking about mine!"

I couldn't make sense of it.

"Is she alive?" I asked.

"Which one?"

"The… wife," I said.

"Yours or mine?" he asked.

"What?"

"Are you asking about your wife or mine?"

"Sandra," I said.

"So you're asking about my wife!"

"What the fuck are you doing here?"

"I'm here to clean up your mess," he said. "You're going to have enough problems when Margaret comes up here. You'll be glad to see me then."

"I'm glad to see you now."

When I opened my eyes, Margaret was seated in the blue vinyl chair next to the bed, the chair reserved for future widows and widowers contemplating their tomorrows. She was half-reading a glossy fashion magazine, wetting her finger before flipping each page with dramatic indifference, her legs were crossed and the foot on top was bouncing.

"How are you feeling?" she asked.

"Everything hurts."

"I'm not surprised," she said. "That was quite an accident. I think the nurse called it a 'humdinger'."

"I don't know who was in the other car. Are they ok?"

"A man was driving. My understanding is he's going to be fine, but they won't tell me much."

"What about her?"

"Oh, you mean Sandra?"

"Yes."

"Well, she got the worst of it. John tells me she has a

broken leg and foot and her hip is dislocated. And a lot of stitches."

I shook my head. "Alive?"

"Yes."

"I was worried."

"You should have been."

After a moment, "I really screwed up, didn't I?"

"Your words," she said and nodded her head.

"My head really hurts."

"Maybe that's some sense being knocked into it."

I didn't get to see Sandra before I was discharged a few days later. Hooper was camped out at the hospital and I didn't want to ask Margaret. Sandra was eventually transferred to Mass General Hospital where she spent about a month. In fact, I haven't seen her in a year since the accident.

A couple days after the accident, Bill called to see how I was doing and to tell me to take as much time as I needed to recover. We'd worked together for the past thirty years, traveling to distant lands, drinking until dawn with every street urchin and ill-mannered cretin imaginable, but he didn't seem to know me. His voice was tinny and distant, hurried, like he was speaking to me from down the hallway, about to make a break for the emergency exit before slithering down the fire escape. "Work will always be here," he said in that cold corporate-ese, an *I wish I had spent more time with my family* kind of way. The second hammer was coming and I knew the hand wielding it was Bill. I, of course, was a shiny, deserving nail.

A few weeks later, an overnight envelope arrived that

required my signature, an official piss off, i's dotted and t's crossed. The enclosed letter thanked me for my years of service and told me how much I meant to the company and explained they'd decided it best for us to end our relationship. Since the accident occurred while traveling for the company, there would be an insurance remuneration. It was signed with black ink in Bill's pretentious, looping hand, likely with the fountain pen I'd presented to him to commemorate his twenty-fifth year with the company.

My first thought was to ring Bill's wife and enlighten her to—where do I start—the lanky stripper in New Orleans, the gambling and debauchery in Macau and Bangkok— well, even speaking of that collective deviance would require a month of unholy Sundays and a scrub brush. Yes, old Billy boy's name was scratched onto the fat man's naughty list and perhaps in even bolder script than my own. I rehearsed my speech to Mrs. Bill, spilling the sordid details of his exploits like a bowl of hot soup on his lap, pausing for her expected reaction, her gasps, the horror of it all. Yes, if my day had come, so had his. I washed my giggling and snorting thoughts down with neat tumblers of Bombay gin and bile. It was so much fun, so invigorating, planning a man's undoing. Perhaps, I thought, I could fashion this inebriated and vulgar creativity into a new profession, a sort of rent a scoundrel for the perpetually clean-handed. Call in old Tommy when you want to ruin a rival's life or turn a baleful tide in your favor, all with your wringed knuckles and sallow ass planted firmly on the couch cushion.

Of course, I didn't call Mrs. Bill, as much fun as it was

to think I might. There was no need to spoil two stews, to tear two family photos down the center on my behalf. My situation, my comeuppance—a fifty-cent-er!—was well earned and long in the making. I just didn't expect it to come from a friend, a fellow heel, despite leaving him little choice. And if our situation were reversed, he the shiny nail and I the mighty hammer, Mrs. Bill holding him down by his scrawny neck, awaiting the cruel thud of justice, I likely would have apologized in the moment of the descending blow. At times I think of Liam the destroyer, now the destroyed, and wonder if our fates were predetermined, ships run aground years apart.

Besides, Aphrodite, despite her voluptuous exterior, is a cruel, fickle old thing who does not take kindly to those who play the spoiler of unions. I earned her wrath a lifetime ago, so forgive my reluctance to drown Billy in the rising bathwater. But, I did hope to win back her favor. Perhaps this night in the tumble of sheets, if I were so fortunate, it would be Margaret, if for nothing else than the convenience of it all.

Yes, that's as awful as it sounds, but it's not to disparage a wonderful woman. I've been sleeping with Susan's ghost for forty years. There has never been another, despite the souls with whom I've shared a bed. Again, that dismissive, petulant tone, but that's not my intent. When I close my eyes, I see her—always her—and she does not allow me the fleeting pleasure of the living. She does not rest and I cannot rest until she might. In her life, she was the tortured soul; now I carry her burden.

There is too much time to think now. This retirement, this forced walk toward the gallows, the loose ends of the binding ropes slapping my flanks raw, onward into Father Time's holding pasture, does not bring the freedom or golden age we were promised when the calendar was flipped to adulthood. The pasture's fence is sturdy, the rungs cannot be scaled, the top lies beyond our strength and ability to hurdle. Here, I remain alone with my thoughts for hours, days without end and there is no more pathetic and lonely and drunken existence.

There was a time when the occasion to contemplate life and love was a great gift, a treat. On one particular windy and cold weekend in March, Susan and I spent nearly two full days in bed musing on life and love, our life and our love. My roommate did not return from semester break and, despite my daily expectations of a new pimple-faced and mealy-voiced roommate arriving at my door, borrowed suit-case stinking of attic and great aunts, an unoiled typewriter in tow, it never materialized. In this, I was blessed with a pasture of my own design, and for this piss-yellow walled pasture, I gladly, even eagerly, gave my wrists to the binding rope.

We, Susan and I, didn't leave the room for entire week-ends at a time. At least, that's the romance of memory, of how it felt to be together, a puzzle where all the pieces fit snugly into place like they'd been attached all along. Or maybe it was true. Save the odd trip to the bathroom or a pajama clad run to the dining hall, hair oiled flat and breath that could choke a horse, I don't think I left the bed other than to change the hissing record on the turntable.

Over the course of the weekend there were several fleshy raps of knuckles on the door—the denizens of the dorm were skilled and unrelenting answerers of the pay phone— and squares of paper with illegible messages scribbled in smeared pencil and blue Bic pen slipped under the door. I always wondered what motivated them, these keepers of the pay phone. On weekends especially, they grew rabid, sprint- ing toward the bell song in giddy, competitive clusters, eager to be the one to lift the plastic receiver and bellow a polite greeting. Perhaps it was anxiety that drove them, for on the weekends lonely high school girlfriends and boyfriends, the ones left behind or snuggled under blankets at far away col- leges, would phone to either profess their undying love or confess to sordid goings-on in their true love's absence.

I ignored them all, refusing to answer the door or read the messages. There was no one I needed, no one worth speak- ing to at that moment. They could wait, all of them. I chose instead to burrow deeper into the sheets and wool blankets, to enjoy the warmth of Susan's body until it was impossible to enjoy it even a millimeter more. I had everything lying beside me, with me, on me. I never loved her more.

New England does not easily surrender its winter, the blue-eyed mistress teases and taunts before she reluctantly departs with one last flirty chill. Throughout the weekend, the lion winds of early March, her last flirt, whistled through the cracked and worn edges of the windowsill and where the window frame no longer formed a tight seal. The radiator hissed and groaned like a stubborn old man lifting too heavy a load, taking in great steamy breaths and releasing them in a futile attempt to keep pace. With our bodies tucked up to our necks under the thick layers of blanket and sheet, only Susan's nose was cold. On a whim, she dipped her icy beak into the pit of my arm, sending me, foolishly, screaming and scurrying out from under the blankets and onto the floor, bare-assed. The cold floor burned the calloused pads of my feet, sending shivers to envelope my entire body. She laughed that squealing, childish, perfect laugh at her own antics and rolled deeper into the blankets.

The cantankerous radiator wasn't the only sound competing with the perpetual sizzle and drone of the turntable. A weekend at Stevens invited an ebb and flow of students and their expectant guests, fueled by cafeteria trans-fats, lousy with gibberish and furious hormones. The sound rose then faded as they approached then shuffled past my door, the sliver of light from the hallway beaming through the bottom of the door interrupted by moments of fleeting shadows. I selfishly wondered if any of them, anyone alive, could ever be as happy as we were in that moment, our middle finger delightfully raised to the world.

When we did sleep, it was always in the same position, her firm back to my front, the curves of our bodies aligned just so, my arm draped over her, one hand gently cupping a bare breast. When she asked why I slept that way, why my greedy hand need always be full, I told her I wanted to make sure her breasts were still there, that they hadn't escaped or been stolen in the night. She laughed, but my fear, my far-fetched premonition that her breasts, and therefore she, would someday be gone, proved prophetic. I wish I had held on tighter, wrapping both scrawny arms around her, pulling her close, then closer still, protecting her. Protecting me.

Around that time, Susan was receiving shock treatments and, over a short period, it appeared to soothe her, to bring a modicum of peace to her never resting mind. I was happy for her, happy for us, happy for me. That weekend, we spun 45s, playing "Baby Come Back" and "We Will Rock You" until the vinyl was dizzy and worn thin, all while drinking room temperature Narragansetts and eating stale pretzels from a greasy cellophane bag. And we laughed deep, ridiculous laughs when she thought Eeyore was a horse.

"He's a donkey," I explained.

"No, he's a horse with a nail holding his tail on."

"It's a pin."

"Yeah, holding his tail on."

"Right, like pin the tail on the donkey!"

"Oh!"

I'd never seen her so happy, full of snorting giggles and foolhardiness, the gifts of youth we long to wrestle from thin air, net and bottle for future use. Then, without warning, a sensation reserved for hopeless romantics, the lolling poem writers of the world with their fancy notebook scrawl and bare feet, began to germinate and fester in the heart of this dullard. I wanted to marry her so we'd be together forever, tethered at the hip and ring fingers. Yes, that weekend I decided I would ask for her hand—how old fashioned—her hand in marriage

I owed Dr. Inslee some gratitude or at least acknowledgment of his progress. His methods, though difficult for me to condone, appeared to improve Susan's psyche and mitigate some of her burden, to leash that ever-present cumulonimbus cloud to a sturdy hitching post.

Susan lived life at full speed, speeding up mountains, sweeping those around her into the euphoria of her wake, only to lose her footing on an unstable rock, smash her chin and tumble down, ass over tea kettle, to the bottom of a ravine. There she lay bruised and bloodied until she found the energy for her next, doomed run skyward.

Over time, the ravine deepened, the walls grew impossibly steep and covered in slippery moss. Emerging from the depths required more energy and resolve each time, a willingness to climb. This continued resolve and willingness, the magical pixie dust that prolongs all life, is eventually exhausted—the when, of course, is impossible to predict. The shock treatment, at least in my uneducated brain, had slowed the progression, preserved some of the pixie dust.

From what I observed, Dr. Inslee was more than a bit slippery. He existed on a different plane of consciousness, aloof and condescending, balanced upon a steaming stew of medical jargon and self-praise. I find doctors of the head and mind often carry an odd spectral glow, a kind of milky halo we mortals fear instills the ability to pass judgment on our insecurities and carnal desires. As my father said once about a man he didn't particularly care for, but wanted to avoid the hurling of insults: "He's a different sort of fellow." The trust, to say the least, was very thin.

Yet, for all the progress made, the welcome appearance of Susie and Sue, by the end of the weekend the crying had returned. There were small sobs that bubbled up from her stomach and convulsed her entire body in tight intervals, bending her forward at the waist and bringing her knees tight to her chest as she gasped for breath. It was soul-crushing to hear, worse to see, the girl with it all, the girl others wanted to be, Aphrodite's reflection fading and blurred. And, worst of all, I was powerless to help.

She couldn't tell me why she was crying—she didn't seem to know herself—something that confused and terrified me and does still to this day. Emotionally limited as I was, I hugged her with all my might until I feared a thunderous crack, a shattering of Eve's ribs. I prayed to whoever might listen, to God, to Aphrodite herself to save her kin. In an instant, she was at the bottom of a ravine.

What is the purpose of mirthful memories when they usher in the melancholy?

16

I never loved Liam, but maybe I could have in a different time and place. It may be that Tom's actions were as much to keep Liam from me and me from Liam as it was to, in his eyes, right a wrong. I had mixed feelings at the time and perhaps I still do today. I didn't hate Liam though I could understand why Tom would. The throwing of stones was something that always gave me pause. I think Liam loved me—he did tell me once—but, like all men, he lusted after Susan. I, of course, loved Tom and he loved and lusted for Susan. It's quite a confusing thing to be nineteen or twenty, contemplating where you stand in the world.

This house gives too much time, too much time to revisit those who are lost and those who are dead. The house itself is almost dead—not in sturdiness, the roof keeps the rain off our heads and the windows allow the light of day, but it lacks a soul. A house, of course, is the sum of its occupants, subject to their whims of kitsch decoration and ever changing moods and taste. How many times can one renovate a kitchen—stovetops and islands, cabinetry undone and rebuilt, floors sanded and stained—before realizing the stubborn sourness lingering in the air is due to the chef's untimely death?

Lily is still in awe of the metamorphoses, our "season of change" she calls it, to the point of throwing herself in front of this or that, a crumbling credenza—is that still a word we use?—trying to save one childhood memory, one cause, like a passionate and single-minded hippie chaining herself to a redwood about to meet the saw. "All we have left is change," I tried to explain to her one afternoon over cold tea and problems of the heart. "There's too much change," she complained.

She was always a bit of a pessimist, a product, no doubt, of a household unintentionally devoid of real, meaningful hope. Ironic, since she was the hope. That's not to say it was a depressed home populated with purveyors of doom and gloom or negativity at every turn. It wasn't. Despite our tendency to share the house (Tom and I) rather than living together, we were cognizant of our effect on Lily. Or at least that was our goal. The truth? This house is the nesting place of ghosts and shadows; those from the past hang over the present and taunt the living. There's no escaping the fact we are the product of our experiences, our loves and losses, our failures and, on occasion, our success. This house gives too much time.

Lily was in one of her moods where the world was caving in around her and the exits were blocked with debris: boulders, fallen trees, immovable objects of that nature. She's an accepter of things, throwing up her hands in a huff of surrender, not one driven to unearth the hidden exit, the one not so obvious, requiring digging and squirming, dirt under the fingernails, when panic ensues. She told me she didn't know how to be with another person, not in the carnal sense, but to exist with others. In her eyes, she'd been alone her entire childhood and now she didn't believe herself good company. The weight of our ignoring each other (Tom and I) had buried her, left her in hiding both in her room and in her mind. Now, when Gary wanted to talk, wanted to watch a movie, even have dinner, the pressure in Lily's head was overwhelming, triggering a feline-like scramble to the dust and darkness of under the bed. The quiet dinners of her childhood were deafening affairs, unspoken and inadvertent torture. Those dinners were that way for all of us.

"Why didn't you and Dad just get divorced? Why are you still together?"

"We'd only make two other people unhappy," I said hiding behind a laugh.

"Sorry, Mom," she said with wide eyes. "I hope I'm not you."

"You've made that quite clear, but you're not me. You couldn't be." I paused a moment. "Your father and I were broken a long time ago. Not by each other, but by circumstances. Guilt is probably the right word. It sounds so melodramatic, I know, but we spend our lives keeping each other intact, keeping each other… alive."

"Why did you have a child?" Lily asked.

My face heated to a rosy swell and hot tears welled at the corners of my eyes.

"Why does anyone have children?" I offered.

Lily frowned.

"We assumed it would give us a purpose, a reason."

"And did it?" she asked.

"Of course it did!" I replied sternly before softening. "At least for a while."

"So having me was just something to keep you busy. Like a hobby," she said and looked off into the distance.

"No," I said softly and shook my head. "Having you was having hope."

The tea had gone cold so I started another pot of water on the stove, getting up from the table so she couldn't see me crying.

"I think we all see our parents as these stoic people who put their heads down and barrel through obstacles. I know I did—my parents always had the right answer or at least pretended they did. But, parents are people with the same doubts and fears as everyone else, they just don't always show them. And your parents in particular, are well… as I said, broken."

Lily was listening, nodding along to the sound of the words, but her attention was elsewhere. She sat dipping a teabag in and out of the cold water, elbow resting on the kitchen table, her slender, blue veined hand lifting and lowering at the wrist, the thin white string pinched tightly between her thumb and index finger. She took a deep, deliberate breath for my benefit, in through the nose, and released it with a dramatic sigh.

"I'm getting divorced," she said without looking up.

"Now I can officially join the fucked-up people. I am you. So much for hope."

It was odd to hear Lily swear. The words smoothly rolled off her tongue, like she was experienced with using them, comfortable, and she'd spent some time honing the delivery. She wasn't a child, she was married off, though in light of the new information this was evidently a temporary state, so I could not deny her adulthood. Perhaps it was simply out of character for her to use such words. I'd spent my life sketching her character, ribbons and bows, yellows, flowers of daisies, violets and mayflowers, lilies, of course. Over time, the charcoal I scraped along the canvas had smudged, blended and blurred, rubbed off on my hand, details erased here and there, evolved and mutated into its own form as it always does. Our lives and loves are not written in ink.

It's also not to say Lily lacked confidence or the weight of the world had crushed her brittle bones or squeezed the life out of her dreams. She and Gary had done well enough, finished their education (the formal bits at least), seen the world, dove headlong into life, crossed things off the invisible list with the oft-sharpened tip of her invisible pencil. Why is it those who have so much are the ones who readily perceive the sting of failure as an absolute?

On the subject of children—for what middle-aged adult doesn't pine for grandchildren—Lily is wholly undecided. At least that's the response I received on the rare occasion I garnered the requisite derring-do to ask her directly. Or, on occasion, when I'm half-drunk and feeling a bit feisty, I might press my luck on the off chance she'll take an interest in sharing. It may be that she doesn't mind talking about it—not the mechanics, of course, but the topic—but minds talking about it with her mother perhaps out of fear the mechanics may be discussed. Lily (like all the children of the world are for their parents) is still my hope for tomorrow.

It's this house again, and me within it and too much time. What is this house but a collection of rooms, smaller than they build today, "quaint and charming" a realtor would say to describe the house with its low ceilings and many doors that hopelessly lead to dead ends. A cottage, I guess you'd call it, a hastily constructed thing where one might spend a holiday, but not a lifetime. The garage was slapped on later, an undignified two staller with mismatched roof shingles and a squat demeanor. Perhaps the previous owners were adding on, expanding their living space to accommodate their growing family. Or, like Tom and I, were intent on putting more air between the occupants.

Whenever I'm feeling sorry for myself, I ask this question: would Liam have been my hope? In some ways, I'd like to think so, but so many things would have needed to be different, so many decisions were needed to change the charted course. In the end, he wasn't who I thought he was.

I'd never given into his advances, the hormone-fueled bouts of physical need, at least not completely or to the extent he wanted. For some reason, I always felt our trysts in the library basement were wrong, like I was cheating on Tom even though Tom wasn't mine. Selfishly, I have to think Liam's drug-fueled seduction of Susan was in part to punish me, to show me that I was missing out, that I could be her if only I'd agree to it. Afterward, the problem, of course, was whenever he approached me, offered to take me to a movie or on a Saturday nature hike through a state forest, all I could see was Susan's bare shoulders bouncing in the back seat and Liam's neck craned to one side, his green eyes staring into mine, the sweet, humid odor of sweat lingering in the air, fogging the windows.

At some point during junior year, Liam began to secretly hone his methodology, his business presentation to young women, making sales and closing deals, providing them with hits of acid then seducing them. This went on for several months until one of them mentioned her experience to a friend. To her horror, the friend had the same experience, under the same method, under the same influence. Further discussions yielded the full extent of his predation, though it's possible there were others. Liam was ultimately charged with six counts of rape and four counts of sodomy. The charming Liam, the boy with the blond curls, the green-eyed monster, spent nine years in prison.

After a lifetime of reflection, those humid summer evenings on the porch swing alone with the gritty sounds of the oncoming night and winter mornings wrapped in a blanket in front of a hissing fireplace, a cup of hot coffee warming my palms, replaying and reshuffling our college days in my head, there is no outlandish shouting of "Eureka!" No reasonable chain of events that twist the future into something more palatable. There is no conclusion, of course, save the one: if I'd given into Liam's advances one evening in the library, opened myself to the possibility that I could love him and, over time, we'd become a permanent couple, not far-fetched in the least, how many lives would be saved? I think we'd have been good together, Liam and I, one monster keeping the other's appetites at bay.

17

Sandra came home today. I watched her through the picture window, largely hidden by the thick blue drapes, the medical van delivering her like so much living room furniture, slowly lowering the wheelchair in a gray electric lift. It was raining and she was uncovered, looking skyward, the rain free to fall upon her face while the driver set the brake of her chair and tried, for what seemed like an hour, to unsuccessfully restore the lift to a position where he could manipulate the van door closed. She didn't seem to mind the rain, maybe it made her feel alive to have the cool droplets on her skin, to be in the light of day despite the overcast sky.

Her hair was pulled back into a tight bun, like an elegant ballerina, but her legs did not move in graceful sweeps and bends, choreographed leaps. Instead, one was braced in rigid metal rods and brackets, forced straight out in front of her, her foot locked straight up and down into a white-socked battering ram. Perhaps that was what she needed to get back into Hooper's good graces, a wheeling start up the oil-smoothed driveway tar, the lanky, blue shirted driver sweating at the handles, company hat flying off the top of his head as his pumping knees worked her up to speed, her stiff, numbed foot crashing through the door, splintering the wood into a thousand shards, pulverizing any resistance.

The driver, of course, wheeled her gently out of the rain, careful to avoid any dips or ruts in the pavement that might bounce her and set off pain in her leg. Hooper met them halfway to ease the front wheels while the driver pulled her backward up the front stairs, the big rear wheels effortlessly bounding the stairs. That would be her life now, easing back into things—her home, her marriage, a sense of normalcy that had eluded her for so long.

She made no attempt to look toward me, for me, as I lurked in the window, hidden behind a glare of glass and drape, a skilled voyeur to the last, an artist cleaving to his last subject in hopes of that elusive inspiration. I assume her focus is on the present, her attention as pointed as that rigid leg, to make peace with her husband, her life as planned and parsed, before the egregious detour. Had she craned her neck around to peek toward me, hoping to catch a glimpse, a flash of movement, a flutter, to wonder if I was indeed a cheering spectator to her homecoming, it likely would have saddened me. That she didn't look may have saddened me more.

Most of all, I miss my drinking partner. My first instinct was to say drinking "buddy", but gin requires a partner, a

committed equal, not a beer-swilling frat brother screaming his displeasure during televised sports or a vodka purist
with raised pinkie at the glass. And, unlike vodka, gin builds
strange and kindred relationships. Now, I have nothing
against vodka and I've been known to dabble in the spirit
on occasion, but vodka does not make demands of the
drinker and, therefore, allows the casual dinner party guest
to imbibe here and there, to take an occasion to turn the
wrist, no questions asked. Vodka is a drink to be enjoyed
in public, under the social lights, while gin offers no such
casualness or frivolity. Gin demands of you a commitment,
a giving of yourself, above all. You have to mean it. And it
must be tasted, front and center, not hidden behind a lurid
combination of juices, sodas and syrups. It's enjoyed in the
shadows, with a wink, when the others have long reached a
restful slumber. Sandra held the gin glass firmly in her hand,
neat, at the ready; she understood what was required. I wish
her well in her recovery, physical and mental, but I know it
won't last.

Is it that time already? I'm meeting Lily for lunch for,
no doubt, more child-parent lecturing concerning daytime
drinking and the like. There's a place she likes to meet, a
dilapidated former clamming shack on the Essex River that's
somehow not yet fallen into the river. The barnacle-laced,
wood support pilings are being slowly digested by saltmarsh
mud causing the building, the shack, to list to one side so
drastically, the oddly narrow and tall water glasses are only
filled two thirds to account for lean. I spend much of the
meal trying, unsuccessfully, to right myself parallel in the

chair, causing a sharp pain in my lower back and sides. Lily says the angle—"slight" she calls it—is what provides the charm of the place; a throwback, unpretentious. To me, it harkens back to a day of shipwrecks and castaways, scurvy and yellow fever, a leaky and ill-wrought vessel with suspect maintenance records and mutinous, black-toothed crew, perpetually on the verge of capsizing and casting us all into the gleaming green monster of the deep. On the bright side, the clam bellies—if you're to believe the menu—are the best in New England, though admittedly, and in spite of the simplistic title, I'm not completely certain what they are. Despite my old-man back and complaints about my shoes sticking to the floorboards and the restrooms reeking like a somber mix of low tide and regurgitating septic, Lily insists this is her favorite place.

Given more time to consider it, the place reminds me of a haughty theme park with a fishing village and nautical motif. There's faux fishing nets hung here and about, and unconvincing plastic or clay lobsters painted dull red, and starfish, shiny schools of tuna and swordfish covered by a thin layer of dust and disinterest, all starving and dying in the nets. There's anchors, ropes, what appears to be a rusting propeller salvaged from a local wreck and a retired, well-worn skiff filled high with ice and dressed with uneven rows of shrimp, mussels, clams and narrow filets of red and pink fish. The main attraction takes center stage in front of the hostess stand: a white-bearded Neptune, a half-naked and life-size being, half-man and half-fish which is, incidentally, half-garish and fully overdone.

One saving grace of a September visit to Essex, Mass is one of nature's crueler creations, the salt marsh greenhead horsefly, is well out of season. Nothing spoils an outdoor meal, or any outdoor activity, like that particular flying and saber-toothed devil. Lily is well aware I'd be impossible to live with if she dragged me there on an afternoon in July, high season for the flying bastards. It's occurred to me that I've settled into a rather well-rounded and eager grouch, the bumpy precursor to becoming an old man. It's long overdue.

"No drinks," Lily says to the pimple-faced waiter before he has the opportunity to ask. "Just water, thank you." She's fired the first shot across the bow.

The waiter shuffles off in an odd, sliding manner, shoulders misaligned with one nearly brushing his ear, one foot dragging behind the other, a necessary evolutionary trait, no doubt, to the angle of the floor and the realities of steadying trays of hot clam chowder. I wonder how long it takes him to correct this deviant posture once his shift ends and he's safely back on dry land. My back begins to ache in sympathetic pangs as I watch him scuttle back to the kitchen.

"So," I say and tap my fingers on the sticky brown table. "Pregnant?"

"No, divorce," she answers, the glass of water moving toward her lips.

"It was a fifty-fifty guess," I say and laugh. "I was close."

"No Dad, that's not close."

Her eyes well up and she stares off into the salt marsh, a thin frown rising up and down. The stench of mud and low tide blows in with a soft wind, but I dare not complain.

There's a light about her today, my Lily. If she'd said it was the glow of pregnancy, I'd have believed her. The sun shining from behind her on the September afternoon lights her delicate features in silhouette, a hidden flower, carving her out of the sun. I wish I'd remembered my camera.

When Lily was little, or at least young, I always had my camera, snapping away, posing her, irritating all. It was something to keep me busy, something to keep my mind off things, something to look at in the future, a reminder that I was supposed to be happy. A ruse to be sure. When you're confused by life you can always hide behind a camera.

"I'm sorry," I say after a few moments.

"You never liked him anyway," she says.

"Well…" I consider lying. "No, I didn't. But you did, so I was ok with him. I had to be."

She looks at me out of the corner of her eye without turning her face. I reach for the water glass out of habit and drink the cool, clean water. It is disappointing.

"I assume your mother knows."

"She does, yes."

The hunchback waiter returns, sliding up to the table with overzealous expectation. He has an oddly high-pitched voice, childlike, like someone is squeezing a small boy just to see what he sounds like. I wonder if he's walking in that strange gait partly to encourage his testicles to finally descend. The laugh and snort at my own secret joke prompts a stern, parental look of condemnation from Lily.

He mentions crab cakes and shrimp cocktail and other things, perhaps. I'm not really listening. Lily, now playing the role of the adult, asks about something or other, maybe even places an order, then sends him scurrying on his way.

"Actually, I didn't want to talk about the divorce," she says in that awful, daughter-to-father voice, at a higher than normal pitch and with that matter-of-fact pace that indicates there's more disappointment forthcoming.

"Oh?" I say as casually as I can muster. In the afternoon heat, condensation droplets form on my narrow water glass, not full, swollen droplets, but rather smug crescents, liquid smiles gleaming and glistening, mocking the soberness of it all.

"It's funny," Lily begins, followed by that verbal tick of hers, the pause, that rope pulled taut at the guillotine's zenith, then a laugh, forcing you to endure a few more seconds of terror before the blood-stained blade's hissing descent, leaving you begging for the drop to end it, head rolling into the basket. She'd make a fine interrogator, my Lily, squeezing out the last bead of juice from the emaciated fruit, the envy of some smirking, ribbon-and-metal-festooned, old world dictator. "I'm more nervous about this than telling you about the divorce."

Lily was born on a perfect New England morning in April. There was a smell in the air, a sweet scent of the world being reborn in green and yellow, the sun spilling over like an overfilled cup, drenching us in warmth. I couldn't stop smiling. Margaret, in her pithy way, said I might hurt my teeth from all of it. Yes, there was too much happiness in our world, even for Margaret's taste. In our lives, there was always another trial, another punishment, another guillotine to keep greased.

In the halcyon days that followed Lily's arrival, we let down our guard, allowed ourselves to dream of her life unencumbered by our failures, unburdened by our insecurities and unshackled from our dour chalkboard of experience. Like the arrival of April, hope was renewed in the spring season. We used to walk Lily for hours, the proud parents, squeaking along in an antique carriage salvaged from my grandmother's basement. It was a hulking thing of wood and metal that one might expect to be pulled by a quarter horse or used to transport an entire litter. People on the street always seemed a little surprised, or perhaps disappointed, to find Lily, and nothing else, in such a grand conveyance. For its part, the carriage bounced gently along on tired, rusty springs and unforgiving metal spoke wheels. The unlikely combination of grandeur and wear lulled her to sleep in minutes.

Those early days were the happiest of the last forty years. We'd forged a family, forcing change. Margaret and I spoke very little, or rather, communicated very little even then. Certainly the day-to-day of life under the same roof requires a degree of speaking, some conversation, but communication is a different beast entirely and our lack of it was likely a factor in our happiness. Until Lily's arrival, we existed in a murky purgatory of love without joy where the sharing of anything more meaningful than the grind of daily life was sacrosanct, saved for those more deserving. Our comfort was in our distance, though for a brief time, we were more.

One summer we rented a cottage on Lake Winnipesaukee. It was our first family vacation and, thankfully, Margaret insisted we go after I'd attempted a last minute reprieve. Why would I not want to go? It appears silly now, of course, but there was always work to be done and family to avoid. That was our way.

"My family goes to the Cape," I explained, clinging to some longstanding and false tradition that the erudite only flock to saltwater.

"This is your family," she explained while running her finger in a circle among the three of us.

The cottage and property were not one for first impressions. Had this been a blind date set in motion by overzealous friends and relatives in hopes of sparking romance, I may have slipped out the back door of the restaurant without regret. The winding dirt driveway, rutted with artillery craters filled with brownish rain and mud, did well to hide the structure behind a hammock of pines and unruly thorn bushes, a feature likely appreciated and encouraged by the neighbors. I stared through the windshield in horror of it all, the storm-stained shingles and sagging roof, window trim in dire need of paint, a lawn consisting of mud and gravel and hopeless tufts of weeds. We'd barely come to a full stop when Margaret turned to me in a preemptive strike, explaining that we were here for the week and I'd better get used to the idea. She likely used more colorful language than I can recall.

The cottage was a damp, dilapidated shack in desperate need of an update and thorough airing out. It smelled, well... old, and indeed it was. It may have been built in the 1920s and used by some middle manager as a rustic getaway from the summer heat of Boston remaining rustic in appearance and spirit. Over the years, there were small, though necessary improvements: a propane stove and not much else. There were two dark-paneled bedrooms, a third which was little more than a walk-in closet, a kitchen littered with 1950s inspired appliances and a small living room with a fireplace, each filled with yard sale quality furniture, all on one floor. The walls were covered with cheeky signs on painted wood, each of which found a way to work the phrase "lake house" into a cheesy, self-reflecting message on your reason for being there.

But, as usual, I was missing point, for despite its ornery appearance, our time spent at that grey-shingled cottage on the lake was magical. As I learned, "heading up to the cottage" had little to do with the broken-down cottage itself—it was simply the vessel, the moderately dry place in which to keep your things. The cottage was about togetherness and the outside. At age five, Lily swam like a fish and spent her entirety of days in the cool lake water, finning about in mask and snorkel one size too large and leaking water on both sides, chasing after schools of minnows, content that this was the meaning of the world. The water was her magnificent playground, gleaming and kissed by the sun, self-healing to the touch, reflecting infinite possibilities, like the life that lay ahead of her.

I spent my days sitting on the dock, bare, pink feet just skimming the water's green surface, taking turns watching Lily and her bright orange life jacket and infinite calls of "watch me" and admiring the seemingly endless parade of motorboats with sunburned captains roaring past and demanding attention, and the calm, smooth rhythm of narrow, green canoes being paddled by braided hair, naturalist types in tan, wide-brimmed safari hats and bagged lunches.

Margaret found a rusted dome grill set on rickety tripod legs that I feared would topple in a slight wind. It was hidden away, tucked in a corner outside near the chimney—banished no doubt, for fear its appearance could somehow tarnish the property's reputation. We threw everything on that rusty grill: sunfish Lily caught on the hook and bobber we found in the half-collapsed shed, thick steaks swirled with fat and wrapped in heavy, white butcher's paper, brawny chicken legs from brawny chickens we drowned in brownish-red barbecue sauce. A cook driven to laughter and madness, I flung down slices of pineapple and watermelon, mushrooms, shrimp and clams. We cooked without fear and, regrettably, without skill. To this day, the sweet, woody smell of charcoal burning down to gray dust still brings me back to that week. For those few days, this was, happily, my family.

There was a small deck, enough for a table and four chairs, most of which was covered by an overhang in the roof. One rainy afternoon, we arranged three of the chairs underneath and sat outside during a thunderstorm. Lily was hardly bothered by the noise or the rain. A coloring book on her lap was entertainment enough and she casually brushed off any stray raindrops as they dotted the greyish-white paper with dark circular stains. Margaret and I sat on either side of Lily, watching the rain over the water, the dark thunderheads commanding the horizon. Lily asked what color crayon she should use next. Margaret and I looked at each other and smiled, our silence saying more in that instant than we'd said to each other in ten years. For that moment, there was hope that we could raise Lily without undue influence, without her having to carry our weighty baggage.

After dusk the lakeside began to cool. With our bellies swollen from dinner and drink and our sun-pink skin radiating heat, the crickets, still hidden from sight, began their violin song and the mosquitos, brazen and single-minded, descended upon us with a sickening bloodlust. The day's black flies, attacking politely in single file, were a relative annoyance when compared to the coordinated and unbearable strafing of the insatiable night flies. The slapping of palm and flesh—an ineffective and hopeless defense, all waving arms and too much effort—was our cue to retire to the living room and a roaring fire. Earlier in the day, I'd located a pile of seasoned hardwood several paces from the shed, cleverly hidden and protected by a heavy blue tarp. I lifted the tarp at one corner, half-expecting to uncover a family of groggy and glassy eyed raccoons or worse, a nest of irritable yellow jackets that would send me scurrying back to the house. Thinking back, it was likely the stash of some soon-to-be-annoyed neighbor, but I paid that no mind and pilfered at will.

When the fire was tall and rolling, hissing and cackling like an old man's throaty cough, I uncorked a bottle of wine. (Wine! The thought is so foreign now.) I found two scratched wine glasses in one of the greasy kitchen cabinets and wiped them clean with a damp dishtowel. Margaret found a dusty and torn copy of Kipling's *Jungle Book* hidden on a forgotten shelf, the cover barely holding to the binding, yellowing pages dog-eared and gritty, and we took turns reading stories to Lily, to each other, in the warmth and flickering light of the burning wood. Lily continued her coloring into the evening and drew loopy pictures of life at the lake, her knees bent, legs to one side as she sat between us on the orange and brown plaid couch, the light of the fire illuminating one side of her face in a yellow glow, the other side steeped in mystery and shadow. As it turned out, the inside of the cottage could hold its own against the outside.

How old were we the year at the cottage, Margaret and I? Thirty-five, thirty-six? We thought ourselves much older, I believe, adults even, driven toward convention, the rascally years of misbehaving well in the rearview mirror. We were parents after all, with responsibilities and a mortgage, lost deep in the trenches, the inevitable fog of career and middle-class dreams, picket fences and PTA meetings. How is it those heavy burdens, real and tangible, seem so light upon reflection, so deftly navigated when compared to the current, refurbished stresses, the relative freedoms of the now?

There was another vacation, a second one, on Cape Cod, perhaps ten years after the cottage, when Lily was deep in the brooding teenage years, all hiss and huff, and I'd discovered gin. Margaret, bless her, hadn't changed. She was not one to fuss or bend to the season: always a smooth, steady drive on a straight freeway. The memories of the Cape, of course, are poor reproductions, amateurish smears of paint when compared to the fine art of my cottage recollections. Recapturing magic is elusive, despite our manufacturings, and my overzealous expectations were held down by the soft parts of the neck, the gloved hand of reality slowly pressing on my windpipe. The Cape and the beach, despite their promise and my braggart's grand predictions, could not deliver a miracle, did not build upon the facade, the illusion of the happy family together at the lake cottage. Had life changed, or was I voluntarily led to the slaughter, reigns hung loose as I ambled toward the barn, suspecting nothing?

All the ingredients for a vacation were there: the well-lit and sand-filled beach house perched above the sand dunes and crashing ocean waves, the greedy mewl of white gulls and scent of sweat swirled with coconut sunscreen. Flip-flops were at the ready, thick-framed sunglasses with impossibly pink plastic rims, bathing suits and sun umbrella. The theater was filled and house lights dimmed. The actors had memorized their lines, throats were cleared, costumes had been fitted and sewn. Yet, when the curtain opened, there was nothingness, a void, a farce, the speaking roles were silent, the silent roles absent entirely. When the reviews were printed, opening night and beyond were an abject flop.

Unsurprisingly, I was ill-suited to the lead role, the debonair family man—perfect posture, chiseled and dimpled chin, head thick with dark, lustrous hair. Instead, I chose the role of a drunken, bumbling, sideshow clown, pissing from the top of the sand dunes, ankle deep in gritty beach sand and wobbling under the light of the stars, who awoke in the cool, humid air of morning, itchy and swollen from sand fleas after spending the night on a wooden deckchair crumpled like a marionette whose strings were severed.

Margaret, her hair tied into a tight bun and shiny spatula in hand, prepared breakfast that morning, whirled knives and pans into sunny-side eggs, thick maple bacon, buttered white toast and potato sliced thin, salted and fried into chips. From the far side of the breakfast table, she asked if my night stone drunk and passed-out on the deck, red, bug-bitten eyelids swollen into slits and hair plastered to one side of my head, had taught me anything. "Probably not," I answered while shoveling a slice of toast piled high with egg into my mouth, bits of egg dribbling onto my shirt, toast crumbs falling onto my lap like a squall of snow. Lily rolled her eyes. All my performance lacked was a throaty belch, index finger extended and pointed to the heavens, and an overt scratching of my crotch. I'd established myself as a perpetual embarrassment, the charming lout, a staple of the wrinkled and gray woman that managed central casting, a role I've failed to relinquish.

The undoing of things was my undoing.

And now, when I see Lily, I fear I've placed all my foolishness upon her, ruined her. Yet, isn't that our role as parents: to impart the wisdom and the pain we've scraped together and earned through sweaty trial and error, squirrelled away across our myriad seasons? Aren't our offspring destined to inherit our worst traits once we've dropped this sack of stones at their feet? Why then are we surprised and disappointed when, despite every moss-covered rock being overturned and landmine dug up and flagged, we witness a mirroring of our lives?

Lily isn't the nervous type. Shy, yes. Introverted, introspective, yes and yes, but one to speak her mind with conviction when in the moment. It feels odd to see her nervous, the table moving slightly as she bounces her leg underneath, her eyes blinking more than required. Breaking the tension, the waiter drops several plates in front us, steaming crab cakes and iced shrimp cocktail, then stands like a peacock, awaiting either our compliments or a dismissal. "Thanks," I say, and a few awkward seconds later, he disappears.

"So, what's going on?" I ask.

"I've started seeing someone," she begins.

"You mean like a boyfriend?"

"No."

"A girlfriend?"

"Uh, no."

'Well, that's all I have," I say and unconsciously push my hands together as if in prayer, resting my elbows on the table. Gray and white gulls mewl in the saltmarsh, menacing each other, splashing after crabs made vulnerable by the changing tide. Two men in black rubber chest waders and wide-brimmed hats dig into the exposed mud with seasoned clam rakes, their gloved hands tossing their prizes into weathered white plastic buckets and quickly covering them with lids as the gulls close in. I learned long ago saltwater, even brackish water, was not my element.

"I'm seeing a psychiatrist," she says while my attention is diverted.

"Why would you do that?" I ask.

"This isn't 1970—things have changed. Everyone sees somebody."

"Not everyone."

"Well, everyone should. Maybe you should."

"What does that mean?" The sweat begins to bead on my forehead.

"It just means everyone needs to get things off their chest sometimes. It might help."

"What exactly do I have to get off my chest?" I ask.

"You're kidding me, right?" she replies and huffs like a spoiled teen.

One of the clam diggers is chasing a gull away from an open bucket, plodding through a few inches of water, swinging the rake and waving his arms, trying to save what little he's collected. This particular bucket is missing a lid and the gulls, not the fools they allude to be, probe and prod it aggressively, testing their luck and awaiting an opportunity.

The waiter returns to the table, his reasonable attentiveness quickly becoming a burden. He smiles and puts his hands together like he too is praying.

"How is everything so far?" he asks, his politeness too much for me to bear.

"Fine," I say.

"Is there anything I can get for you?"

Lily's sitting back, deep into her chair to maximize her distance from me, arms crossed tight on her chest, staring at me above the tip of her nose, expecting a terse and rather rude comment to fall from my lips. I don't take the bait.

"No, thank you," I say behind a forced smile of closed mouth and lips pressed together. "We're all set for the moment."

The waiter looks at each of us without moving his head, his eyes sliding across his face toward Lily, to me, then back to Lily again. With a small nod of his head while his body lists to one side, one shoulder pinned to his ear, he ambles away yet again.

"Listen," I say. "These people kill people. Believe me, they kill people and destroy lives."

"And what if they also save people? What if they save me?"

"Do you need to be saved?" I ask.

It's Lily's turn to crane her head and stare off deep into the marshes, to find a void, an emptiness in the afternoon, and climb into it, to practice the art of avoidance I've spent a lifetime mastering. The men in rubber waders and hand rakes have disappeared from view and the gulls have dispersed, but tourists in bright yellow kayaks have wandered into the marsh, only to become stranded in the mud, exasperated, struggling in the shallow water of low tide. Lily's eyes begin to redden and swell, her face is wet with the warm salt of tears. The droplets run down her freckled skin in single file, blazing glimmering trails to follow, balanced momentarily on the sharp upwardly-turned ridge of her top lip, then falling onto the table in light, audible taps.

"Dad," she says slowly, with the stoic comfort of a child grown sure and strong with the march of the seasons, the maturation of years. "You're not going to lose me."

"Ok," I say and nod, my eyes closed tightly. "Ok."

18

For me, smells, scents, take me back in time, back to a specific memory long buried deep in my brain, tucked away in a dusty crevice or behind a deposit of lipid fat and calcium. An unexpected whiff of vintage cologne or Pall Mall cigarettes sends a long lost uncle or aunt back to me in an instant, sitting beside me here, erasing a thirty-year absence in an instant. The smell of a campfire brings me to the house at the lake with Tom and Lily one perfect week in summer. Most times, I let myself enjoy the recollections, remembering the good times and, I assume, blocking out any bad. That's the way memories are designed: positive, happy memories are protected, encapsulated in a thick, pliable shell while the negative energy is shed like neutralized virus, mitigated over time until there's nothing left.

There's one scent that brings back feelings of regret and fear and work not yet done. Apples, more specifically, apple shampoo gives me the most trouble, makes me sick to my stomach. Over the years, I've learned to avoid being exposed to anything apple, giving wide berth to the fruit section in the supermarket, pushing the carriage in unnecessary and elongated loops is one of the more overt methods. Holding my breath in the shampoo aisle is another little trick. The scent is more difficult to avoid than one might think. Slices of the prolific fruit turn up wallowing on top of innocent lunch salads and dripping as overflow from the miniaturized straws of juice boxes stuck to the hands of the neighbor's unsuspecting five-year-old.

The apple smell, the memory itself, was from the last time I saw Susan. It was sophomore year on the last day of finals. She'd already packed up her room and had stopped by to help me with what little packing I had left. I'd already stuffed most of my belongings into several green vinyl suitcases and assorted canvas duffle bags, and was removing posters from the wall. For those looking forward to going home, posters came off the wall early, making the room less like home in preparation for departure. For me, they stayed on the walls until the very end, the last possible moment—I never wanted to leave my dorm room.

Susan was wearing her staple: tight flair-bottom blue jeans with a short-sleeve knit sweater, solid white with blue and red bands on the sleeves. Her hair was freshly washed and distinctly smelled like apples. We planned to see each other over the summer, hang out every week or at least at parties, meet each other's friends from home, that sort of thing, so I thought it a bit odd that she wanted to help me pack. I assume her arrival meant she wanted to talk, that there was something on her mind.

She sat on the bed, legs crossed, watching me pack with the vague detachment of a supervisor who believes her talents are best suited for an assignment two rungs up the corporate ladder.

"Oh, I love him!" she said when I removed the thumbtacks from a *Saturday Night Fever* poster and began to roll it up. Then: "Tom wants to take me to Maine next weekend, some place called Marginal Way."

"Never heard of it," I said.

"What do you think he's up to?" she asked.

"Why would he be up to anything? Is it strange that he'd want to take you somewhere for a weekend?"

"No, I guess not," she said before being distracted. "Those suitcases are fancy. You don't see that color green every day. Looks like a mint lollipop."

"The tackier the better!" I said. "That's my motto. I think they're the suitcases my parents took on their honeymoon, so they're some kind of gaudy family heirloom. Lucky me."

"Listen," she began. "I wanted to ask you if you still had the pill Liam gave you."

"Why?"

"I could use the distraction about now."

"Yeah, I still have it. Are you sure you want it?"

"There's some shit going on, you know, and I… I may not be ready."

"Ready for what?" I asked.

"I don't know, the weekend away, all of it. I'm having a rough time."

"Is there anything I can do?"

"Yeah, you can pass along Liam's pill."

"Sure, no problem. It's in a plastic bag in my jewelry box, still on the dresser."

"I'm sorry," she said.

"Sorry for what?"

"All of it, everything."

"We're friends, you don't need to apologize. How's it going with the treatment?"

"Maybe more harm than good. I really don't know. The whole thing is fucked up."

She took the plastic bag from the jewelry box and zipped it into her small tan leather purse then opened her mouth to say something, but there was no sound.

A moment later she asked, "When are you getting picked up?"

"My parents are coming in the morning, around eight o'clock. What about you?"

"Tomorrow, noon maybe. My mom is driving up with my little brother. I think she wants him to get used to the idea that he's expected to go to college, that sort of thing." She pushed her hair behind her ears with both hands, smiled and nodded, almost as if to say, "My little brother is growing up."

"Patrick, right? How old?"

"Yes, Paddy. Eight. The little prick," she said and laughed, her attention trailing away from me again, her voice fading. "Nah, he'll be alright, he's a good kid."

She lay down on the bed and swept her arms and legs across like she was making a snow angel, folded the comforter over her legs and feet, and closed her eyes. "I love this bed. I may fall asleep."

"How about some ABBA?" I asked.

"That would be divine," she said in a breathy exhaustion, a long steady exhale whistling thinly through her nose. "Do you know why I love this bed?"

"No," I answered.

"Because I can hide in it. When I'm in this bed no one is looking at me funny and wondering if I'm normal or a fucking crazy today. No one is asking how I'm feeling and tilting their head like a confused dog." She let out another long exhale and smiled for a moment.

I'd yet to pack the albums, packing in order of non-important to essential would have left music and stereo last, even after the posters. I removed the LP from the sleeve and paper jacket, placed the record on the turntable and gently set the needle. I turned the volume dial low and let her fade away, one breath at a time. The hiss and crackle of the LP, the sound crisp and light, slowly filled the emptiness of the room, cascaded into every crevice and void like a rolling morning fog.

Her rest was deep and determined, her stomach rising and falling in perfect pace and rhythm, her lips slightly parted, her eyes buried under ivory lids, perfectly still. I've wondered if she'd planned to fall asleep in my bed all along. After all, as she mentioned, my room was a safe place, free from judgment and the prying eyes of men, absent of the stigma of her breakdowns. She moved slightly, a twitch only, when the first side of the record ended, the needle exhausting the grooves and sliding over the smooth frontier. I turned it over with great care, balancing it between the tips of my index fingers and using the fleshy tips of my thumbs to rotate it without fingerprints.

Most of the girls in the dorm had emptied their rooms for the semester, hitching rides with those fortunate enough to have cars on campus or endured the embarrassment of their parents arriving in gas guzzling sedans or worse, bench-seated family station wagons embellished with wood paneling and white wall tires, shouting orders back and forth between uncomfortable hugs. The dorm, as you might expect once it lost its boisterous inhabitants, possessed a medieval quality, an empty, echoing castle that at all times of the day, even when the sun cut full, could use more light, more sound, more joy. I didn't like the idea of spending even one night alone, so though the castle remained silent and still, it was not peaceful and I didn't mind the company. My room and comfortable bed provided sanctuary; Susan's presence was mine.

Around 10pm, a voice echoed through the hall, Tom's voice, calling me, calling Susan. I opened the door and went out into the hall to meet him. It wasn't odd for Tom to call my name rather than the more conventional knocking on the door—he of course knew which room was mine—he was trying to avoid my roommate, Vicki. Vicki had a thing for Tom, a girl's crush, and there was little interest in hiding it.

Vicki was a tall Midwestern type, fair skin and freckled

arms, straight blond hair halfway down her back often pulled into a loose ponytail, a farm girl with her mother's friendly, high-pitched twang and her father's thick hands. She spoke very fast, like she needed to move on to something pressing and had only a few moments to wrap up the current conversation. Vicki was pleasant enough as roommates go, and we got on fine, sharing a room for two years despite running in different social circles. Mostly, we coexisted in a serene cohabitation.

Other than borrowing a few albums and, on occasion, a sweater, the only thing we had in common was an affinity for Tom, though, unlike Vicki, it was something I could scuttle under the rug. When Tom was around, in our room, in the cafeteria, at a party, she gazed at him open mouthed in a kind of fawning, breezy wonderment, like a boy stares at his favorite baseball card while dreaming of the day he'll play in the big leagues or a grown man admires his red, mid-life crisis convertible after applying a second, unnecessary coat of wax, his arms crossed in front of him, chin forward, as he leans back ever so slightly.

Vicki never said much to Tom other than quick, social niceties, an unintentionally breathy "hello" or "how are you, Tom"—something that really meant "I see you there." There was nothing obscene or out of place in her actions, there was simply a twinkle in her eyes that made Tom uneasy.

"Vicki went home," I said before Tom could ask. He shook his head and opened his eyes wide, his mind too cluttered or strained to accommodate even one grain of sand more.

"Susan with you? She blew me off." It was odd to see Tom (perpetually even keeled) rattled, his eyes staring into the emptiness of the hallway.

"She's asleep."

"What the Hell? That's all she does is sleep."

"That's what people do when they're depressed," I said.

"Depressed? I thought she was cured. Dr. What's-His-Ass cured her, didn't he?"

"Listen, I don't know, but this approach ends badly for you. You know that."

"I know, I know," he said and took a breath. "It's just, it's hard to deal with sometimes."

"Yes, it is," I said. "But this is what you signed up for."

"I don't know about that," he said and shook his head. "But, anyway, when you heading home?"

"Tomorrow."

"Me too. We'll get together soon though, right?"

"Yes, of course. I'll call her, we'll come up a plan."

"Ok, great. Thank you," he said and hugged me.

"For what?" I asked. He didn't answer, but buried his face into my collarbone, resting it there for what seemed a minute.

I was reluctant to wake her as I'd never seen her at such rest—the smooth, rigid face of a mannequin, at once relieved of troubles and recaptured of innocence, a babe again, free to discover the world. The storm, the whirling tornado—much of it her own doing—had passed, the clouds swept beyond our sight, if only for a moment.

When she woke, she looked at Tom with a pensive

disillusionment, like she assumed his arrival meant they would take up whatever unpleasant discussion she'd fled, draining the positive energy she'd shrewdly pilfered from the evening.

"Have fun in Maine," I said to Tom in what I assumed was the best flirty voice in my arsenal, the word "Maine" elongated and higher-pitched on the end for effect. He looked at me with the wide eyes of a confused child, his eyebrows crunched together like I knew something either he didn't or I shouldn't.

I wished I'd hugged her before she left.

That night, I wrestled insomnia, slipping in and out of its calloused clutches, eyes unable to rest, breathing in the moist night air through my nose, the sweet scent of apple shampoo rubbed deep into the pillowcase. Was it that night I first lost the ability to sleep, to leave consciousness behind and keep the running thoughts at bay, to rest? I hadn't considered the when, only the why. To this day, sleep remains elusive, relegated to twenty-minute catnaps and brief moments of dreamy confusion despite a whole night's commitment to bed. Medication helps, those drowsy capsules filled with colored syrup, but they leave me feeling like I've cheated the night of my conscious presence, avoided the torment that will be double the next time.

With Susan gone, I felt lonely for the first time in my life, fear for the first time. Sounds came from outside the dorm window, sounds of an intimate and complete darkness, maple branches scratching along the glass like squeaks from a family of mice as the wind blew out of the north;

while faint, unidentifiable howls echoed in the distance. What specters and demons lay on the other side of the pane, patrolling their night watch, lurking in wait, claws bitten sharp, for a warm, blood-swollen victim, soft and doughy with indifference, a lost sheep? They chuckle to themselves, these toothy creatures of the nocturne in grumbly, low waves we often mistake for rolls of thunder on the horizon. And they drool in anticipation of the clank and whir of chains and a thump of lumber, the castle drawbridge being lowered before a stout, plodding carriage, painted in lacquer red as blood, is sent on its final journey, vanishing into the budding apple orchard. I worked myself up into a lather, feet kicking, nestled between sweat-soaked sheets and a throbbing migraine, the gray light of a crescent moon flickered through the leaves of the red maple gargoyles, alternating shadow and light through the window sheers. Yes, fear itself.

Weeks later, I rummaged through my wicker hamper of unwashed clothes and found the pillowcase from my dorm room, still fresh with her scent of apples, strands of curly hair still clinging, the last vestiges of her existence refusing to hide. I'd like to say I wasn't looking for the pillowcase in the fermenting pile of laundry—hastily stuffed into the hamper and almost forgotten, the one I swore to my mother twice over had been washed and folded on day one—but I was. I sat on the floor of my bedroom, bare footed and legs crossed, holding the fabric close against my nose and mouth, pulling her essence in, the tears warm on my swelling cheeks. I doubled over and fell onto the thick wool area rug, the coarse hair against my face, my knees raised to my chest, a long strand of auburn curly hair stuck to my lips. I needed to sleep and I needed Susan with me, just the once more.

There was one time we took Lily apple picking. She was maybe five or six, that curious and magical age where children are old enough to be amazed by the natural world and your ability to summon it at will, while young enough to still love you. They can experience joy at a mud-covered farm, the choking stench of horse manure lingering in the greasy, humid air, unruly stalks of yellowish hay sticking to your boot or visiting a low budget zoo hosting small cages of chubby native gray squirrels, their fluffy, pipe-cleaner tails twitching, their cheeks stretched full with feed and, next to them, mischievous raccoons lounging about, handsomely dressed as train robbers, perpetually awaiting the next heist. Even at home, they can watch a poorly assembled birdfeeder for hours, content to count the robin red-breasts, the scurrilous screaming blue jays and soul-carrying cardinals, then give you the biggest, deepest hug as a thank you, even if you need to ask for it.

Lily wore a flowered dress and buckle shoes to pick apples, a pink bow high in her hair. Once loose in the orchard, she ran from tree to tree, darting under shaded canopies, vanishing into shadow dappled with sunlight, laughing wildly, intent on tasting every apple she could reach. Tom was in close pursuit, snapping pictures with a monstrous SLR camera he was learning to control, barking on about f-stops and shutter speeds and other nonsense. Soon, her dress and shoes were green with grass stains and caked in brown mud. I was too distracted to notice. The September air, heavy with the scent of apples and fading summer, overwhelmed me in minutes. I sat under an apple tree, a Cortland, in the middle of the orchard, paralyzed, my head aching, my forehead tight against my knees, Lily's laugh fading in the distance. Such is the power of scent.

Soon after Susan's funeral, my mother took the film from my 110 Pocket Instamatic and had it developed at the local pharmacy. She knew, despite the pain of the moment, we would grow to appreciate the memories we'd captured, lanky, naive students in casual poses and tight clothes, carefree and mostly invincible. There were three or four twenty-four exposure cartridges I'd shot over the course of the year, the prints packed in a shoebox and, in the whirl of the next few weeks, forgotten. I still have them, most of them at least, in a forty-year-old shoebox, brown and covered in dust, tucked on the top shelf of my current bedroom closet. On more than one occasion, I've considered placing them in a photo album—do people still do that?—perhaps doing my best to set them chronologically, but Tom thought it best to keep them "free," something Susan could never quite accomplish.

The paper prints are poor quality, edges curling upward and frayed, the images fading by the hour, smudged with thumbprints and coated in grease. The photos shot indoors are mired in flash shadow and murky brown clouds from the chemicals used in the printing process, a translucent silt in which our memories are forever encased. In my mind, the seventies always had a reddish hue, a rosy glow, in no small part due to these pictures. Some of the prints are inexplicably folded in half or crumpled in sections. The wide-angle lens and narrow film of the Pocket Instamatic did little to flatter its subjects in either color or focus—hammering us flat against the harsh background, blended in spectral layers. Yet, there we are—blurry faces and glowing pupils coupled with the grainy rusts, yellows and browns of the decade's fashion that are not easy on the eye. What were we thinking? Still, I'm grateful for having the good sense to bring the camera.

The day Lily came over for lunch to tell me about her psychiatrist, she asked about Tom, Susan and our college days. She must have been searching for ways to understand her father, understand me and, as such, shed some light on her own life. She'd changed her hair—cut short into a confident bob that swept past her eyes when she turned her head quickly—and bought new shoes. She understandably hesitated before mentioning the psychiatrist, but eventually found the courage to speak freely. I offered only encouragement, keeping the door to my basement filled with anxiety, latched tight and secure. She'd taken a risk coming to me (and I assume her father), shown immense maturity and a willingness to work through her angst, to find a way to be better, if one existed. I thought it time she see the photographs. I thought it time I see the photographs.

"I have something to show you," I said.

I fetched the brown shoebox from the bedroom closet, stretching on my toes and extending my fingertips to reach the high shelf, blew dust off the top, then sat with her at the kitchen table. She'd cleared the table of lunch plates and put on a pot of coffee, settled in for the afternoon, intent on connecting some of the dots. The box landed on the table with more heft than I expected, a sort of grumbled thud, the memories grown heavy with age and contempt of being ignored. There were more than I remembered.

Lily reached into the box with a childish delight, like they were valentines collected in her first grade class, seizing a handful of pictures in ways I'd never allowed myself. I may have gasped, but if I did, Lily was too preoccupied to notice. She hadn't done anything wrong, of course, and perhaps I treated the photos as something too fragile, too sacred, like the memories were one time use only and would slip through my fingers and into oblivion the moment I touched them. But what are memories if they can't be shared? What will be lost to time might yet be preserved if there is willingness. Didn't we owe that to Susan?

"What's this one?" she asked, flipping a photo in front of my face, a sheepish grin hammered ear to ear.

"That's me and your dad—I think you knew that—I'm assuming at a fraternity party. Maybe sophomore year?"

"Is this your room? It's groovy!" She laughed while studying another photo. "What's with the posters? Is that *Saturday Night Fever*?"

"It is," I said. "It was very popular." I heard my justification and my stoic mom voice bubble to the surface.

"I'm sure it was."

"What about that one? ABBA?"

"You know your seventies history," I said.

She continued to flip through the prints, taking the one on top and placing it at the rear of the stack in her hand. I watched her studying them, each one a small, die-cut puzzle piece that might bridge a gap in knowledge or connect her in a minute way to her father and I.

"Look at you, Mom, smiling! Every picture. You were so happy."

"Not every picture, I took most of them."

"Well, every picture you're in. Look at this one—big smile, love the top. You were hot!"

"What nineteen-year-old isn't hot?" I asked, but Lily was too busy studying us to answer, pulling the aging prints closer to her face, tightly pinched between her thumb and index finger, her thoughts wandering far away before snapping back, a wide, involuntary grin stretching her mouth, all teeth and gums.

"Dad is happy, too! Oh my God, he was such a ham! Skinny and a tight t-shirt, holy shit. No surprise he's holding a beer. This is a crack up—we should have done this long ago!

"I assume this is Susan," she said while holding a picture of Susan sitting in a purple beanbag chair at the student union, hair blown back in wings, a devilish half-smile and eyes looking past the camera. "She was beautiful."

"Yes, she was. I think your father took that one."

"And her and Dad were an item? Together?"

"She was the love of his life."

"Mom." She paused and put the picture down on the table. "I think that's you."

"I'm afraid not."

"Why would you say that?"

"I was his friend—we were friends," I said and opened my palms and spread my fingers in that sort of slow the madness way. "He didn't look at me the way he looked at her or even the way I looked at him. I couldn't compete with Susan, no one could. She had this gravity all around her, pulling everyone in, pulling everything toward her, like the sun. People just wanted to be around her—she made them smile and feel alive."

"It's ok to cry, Mom," she said, echoing the sentiment I'd expressed to her in the confines of her bedroom during countless conversations in her adolescence, the soft yellow light of her ballerina lamp casting our oversized shadows on the walls, our orange tabby, Mr. Cheddar, curled into a tight circle at the foot of her bed. There were days she worried her nose and feet were too big, then too small, seldom average enough and somehow never much like the perfect features adorning the rest of her friends. And, more recently, when she confessed her troubles with Gary, her tears warming my shoulder, makeup smeared in flesh-colored clouds on my blouse while she wore herself out, blustery and buried deep in a rare hug. Now, how soon our children become our parents, their soggy diaper becomes our diaper, damp and weighty, and the myriad rules we've spent a lifetime con-cocting become their rules we're now asked to follow. To an outsider, this tipping point, the handing off of the paren-tal baton is often easy enough to identify—a health issue arises, difficulty walking or impaired memory, breathing while tethered to an oxygen tank or simply a questionable adherence to a medication schedule after a disappointing doctor's visit. I like to think my moment of need proved more subtle, but no less a surrender to time and life's circle.

In the corner of the shoebox tucked under the photos was a tightly folded square of thin, pinkish rose-colored fabric. Despite its age, it held the color remarkably well. I'd forgotten it was in there. Lily picked up the dense square and inspected it, turning it over, then back, rubbing it between the skin of her thumb and index finger, her elbow on the table for support.

"What's this?" she asked.

"Does it smell like anything?" I asked.

Lily brought it to her nose. "No, I don't think so."

"It used to smell like apples, like Susan's shampoo."

Lily smelled it again. "No, nothing." She held it in front of my nose. "I can't smell anything either."

"What happened to Susan?" she asked.

"She died."

"I know she died, but, I mean, how did she die?"

19

Everyone stared at me like the haughty, petulant star of a morbid documentary on a serial killer or the golden, newly ordained pseudo-celebrity with perfect eyebrows and high cheekbones, thrust into a sleazy tabloid limelight for winning a coveted sweepstakes—the last person to see Susan alive. Their eyes burned words of derision into the back of my skull as they jockeyed for position behind me. Friends, family, neighbors, teachers, former coaches, beady-eyed Liam, the fucking psychiatrist, all of them. They came to see her, to pay witness to the final resting place of the magical girl of infinite happiness and infinite despair. And they came to see the twisted, wretched boy with pale skin and a boy's sparse whiskers, crocodile tears sliding down his pitted cheek, dark droplet circles staining the collar of his gray, off-the-rack wool suit. Whispers of why and how. She was the girl who had it all, of course. Whispers of did he or didn't he. In the seething whirl of death and the funeral for my love, my shirt damp with sweat and clinging to my skin, my nose dripping like a faucet, even I was no longer sure. I missed her more than life.

A funeral for the young is never a celebration of a life well lived or a magnification on a generation renewed and upcoming. It is a sickening affair of lost potential and unfulfilled dreams, toppled dominoes run through with a hollow sword, left wallowing in a nothingness that resists being molded into something promising or, at least, less painful. In the moment, there is never enough time for goodbyes, the suddenness of it all takes center stage of the tragedy, the spotlight focused on a lone empty chair left vacant by the full cast, costumed and powdered, minus one.

Prior to this day, I'd only been to one funeral in my life, my father's, when I was twelve. Back then, the entire affair was done behind the scenes, without me, surely at the direction of my mother who needed to focus on something (in this case my deprivation) to keep her sanity. My father, as I learned later, was an old-school drinker in full operation back when you should have known better, but it was far from a prerequisite. He had a penchant for smoky, dank social clubs—"buckets of blood" he called them—and the whiskey and women available in great quantities in such untrendy locales. In the end, his liver became full-up and could no longer stay the siege. I think in the end my father, whatever his reasons, just wanted out. My mother cried for six months and probably six more months that she hid from me, buried deep in her pillow and her television stories.

Margaret was standing with her mother and father,

huddled close together in a scrum for shelter, her father's arms wrapped around his pack. We spoke on the phone until 4am the night before, me curled into a tight ball and deep into the bed sheets, her likely the same, tossing through memories of Susan like gritty, burning shots at a bar. Still, I felt like I hadn't spoken to Margaret in years, decades. Her face was foreign to me, a stranger in my insular world, yet she was the only one left who knew me. And she was the only remaining person that I knew.

Despite my mother's insistence, I hadn't showered in days.

Susan's father, Mr. O'Malley, could barely hold himself steady, rocking back and forth like a boat docked in a gale wind, lurching and defeated, his legs abandoning him. I thought he might throw up. He was buttoned high into his Sunday clothes, starched white shirt and dark gray suit, black wingtips shined with care, clothes never intended or imagined for an event of such weight. He had a thick, Middle Eastern dictator moustache that, had he been an entertainer from a bygone era, might have been a wide smear of black grease paint instead of heavy whiskers, black with only a hint of gray. This moustache, during his usual mirthful mood, bounced around on his top lip like a mink in full sprint, only resting for a moment between words when he raised a glass of Irish whiskey, neat, to his lips. He was a fine man, one who had always treated me well, but this day he was quiet, the mink still and forlorn. He was unsure where to cast his eyes, bouncing from the Priest to the casket, the flowers and above the mourning flock who'd gathered. His anger, at God perhaps or the surviving flock itself, pushed forth in a ridged scowl. He saved his most sinister glare for me, his head hung low and loose, his neck disconnected from his body like an invisible rope were tied to a cloud to support its weight, his wet eyes peering over his nose, both contemptuous and sympathetic. I can't blame him. Was I the villain or the victim? An enabler or reluctant hero? Was he really giving me a death stare or was I insufferable and paranoid? Either way he was unlikely to ever forgive me as I would never forgive myself.

Mrs. O'Malley was in shock, eyes wide and mouth frozen while forming the letter O—the poor thing, her life twin stolen away. Her eyes were swollen and black underneath and all color had drained from her skin like a stock black and white image from the silent films. I suppose we were all in shock. The movies always show the grieving dressed in black, those left behind unable or unwilling to live in a world with hope. While searching for somewhere to direct my running thoughts, sliding my eyes among the gathered while my head remained still, I realized it was true—people were dressed primarily in dark colors. Are we not supposed to run toward the light? Shouldn't we be wearing white at a funeral? Should we not be cheering in home team colors for our loved one's purest entrance into Heaven?

Mrs. O'Malley distracted herself by comforting young Patrick, draping heavy arms around him and pulling him deep into her dark lace shawl. If he was willing or if she had her way, she would have formed a lace cocoon around him and sealed him away from the world until such time it became a better place, a fairer place. She guarded him, Paddy, with unwavering dedication and fierce will, I imagine, until the day she herself died.

How old was she then? Forty-five, fifty? Younger than I am today to be sure. She had more faith in me than Mr. O'Malley or at least convinced herself to believe in me, the poor fool. When our eyes met from a distance, over the casket bared to the day, I sensed she felt sorry for me—me the pathetic, broken soul, an abandoned dog, glassy eyed and defeated, left caged and shivering at the city dog pound. Indeed I was. If nothing else, she'd seen the way I looked at Susan and gave her all of me, and knew my heart.

How was I to know how they felt, Mr. and Mrs. O'Malley? I, of course, was too busy with me, the selfishness of the moment, my pain and my loss and my life and my Susan. There was, of course, some understanding on my part—wait, understanding is too utilitarian a word. There was some sympathy on my part—we, all of us, had lost her. Now, as a parent, I can't fathom their despair.

When Lily was born, I wrote a letter to the O'Malleys and included a photograph of her in the carriage handed down from my grandmother. The antique carriage was all springs and metal with great spoke wheels that squeaked despite my never ending attempts to grease them. Lily looked like a child from the 1930s wrapped in a heavy, crochet blanket and a pink bow in her hair, while buried deep in the high-sided basket. Margaret and I debated sending the letter, weighing the potential reception of our message—were we sharing a gift, life renewed and our great pride or providing an unnecessary reminder of that which was lost? The O'Malleys wrote back a heartfelt congratulations in Mrs. O'Malley's looping cursive and included a phone number and offer to meet us for lunch if we were ever in the neighborhood. Like many things in my life that I now regret, I practiced the art of proactive avoidance.

I was standing near my mother when Margaret took my hand at the funeral, folding a gentle palm into mine without looking at me. I hadn't seen her make her way toward me, but I was glad to have her at my side. The spring sun was warm against my cheek and we stood together in the damp grass, our shoes slightly darkened, and planted firmly on the ground. A bird, maybe a sparrow, sang a sad song in the distance, perhaps not unaware of our despair. I wanted to ask Margaret, to whisper in her ear, "What do we do now?" How selfish a thought it seemed then, placing us at the center of things, but I have come realize it was not so selfish—our center was forever lost, torn apart at the seams. We knew Susan's gravitational pull, the very fabric of our existence, despite our clawing and pleading, would fade over the coming days and months and years. We were, or soon would be, rudderless and desperate to find our way. Odd to think now, how our standing together, ready to catch each other should one faint or weaken or be in need of comfort, would extend throughout our lives, despite our reluctances.

The Priest, a listing, disheveled fellow with chipped, gray teeth and a hangover, waved a crooked finger toward Margaret and I, calling us over once the casket was lowered into the dark earth, but before any soil had tarnished it.

He handed us red roses with tree-trunk thick stems, one each, our love, to toss down six feet, a fleeting final gesture. When the roses left our grasp, Mrs. O'Malley released a heart-breaking wail, a cruel trick played upon this fine woman, and the others followed in a rolling wave. Margaret could not keep her eyes and mind off young Patrick and she began to shake uncontrollably at my side. I placed my arm around her waist and pulled her close; she sank into my chest.

Vicki, long my admirer, was standing with a group of students I recognized, but didn't know by name, eyes squinting in the sun and freckled face straight forward, chewing on her upper lip, her skin pink and swollen. Yes, even Vicki, ever a kind word and a wry smile, a perpetual sparkle in her eye, would never see me in the same light again. It's hard disappointing people, that wrenching and twisting of the stomach—dry mouth and bad breath. But not hard in the sense of doing something that disappoints them—showing up late or not at all, lying, cheating and overall selfishness. That's the easy part, a boy's life, and often accomplished twice over before lunch. What I mean is being presented with their disappointment, being the actual disappointment and acknowledging the damage done. Worst of all, due to an action, or almost as often, inaction, feeling, knowing things will never be the same. And there are no corrections to this despite our secret and desperate wishes. Before that day, powered by my insecurities, I never thought I would miss the ego and chest inflating attention of Vicki, the unearned love. Things would never be the same.

Inevitably, there came the moment to face the O'Malleys—Mr., Mrs., Paddy. I'd avoided it until the day of the funeral, only partially on purpose, cowardly. I wasn't volunteering to face them, and as you might imagine, I was reluctant. In the whirlwind of her death, I supplied their address to the police, still burned into my memory: 75 Silas Rd, Petersham, Massachusetts. The police, some ruddy sergeant or other, polished metal badge and black boots, handled the official call though I imagine no amount of sensitivity training and crisis management certificates truly prepares you for the moment—if they even had that sort of thing in those days. Even today, I struggle with whether I should have also called them, reached out in some way. But what was I to say that they didn't already know? What would change? Susan was gone and I was not.

The protracted slog of age informs me I should have called the O'Malleys and expressed my sympathies. Wisdom or guilt, I have difficulty recognizing the difference. Contacting them, acknowledging my sorrow and their sorrow was the responsible thing to do, mature and polite and necessary. But what twenty-year-old is responsible and mature and polite and necessary? And where was I in the hours and days that followed? Tucked under my mother's feathered wing, limbs twisted into the nest's soggy bed sheets, stained pillowcase pounded flat in the middle by furious fists and forehead, wondering if my life too had ceased. There's no describing such unmitigated despair and no one, save the O'Malleys and Margaret, could measure it. I was a lost soul treading water, tiring, my muscles burning with acid with every attempt to remain on the surface, my body sinking below the waterline, mouth filling with warm brine. I was lost to it.

Mr. O'Malley grabbed me by the shoulders, one dense hand on each side. I fluttered loosely like a marionette, bouncing in his grasp, unsure where I was to be directed, to what ends. I was rubber, boneless and disconnected. The day brought too much sun and not enough shade and my head was stuffed full of fog and allergies. I thought I might collapse. He pulled me in close—a hug, tight and muscular—his thick whiskers rough against my sallow face. He asked me how I was doing. Not well, I told him. He shook his head and squeezed heavy folds into the skin of his forehead, exhaled in a brief, fatherly disappointment and released me, casting me back into the gleaming blue-green of the sea. He had enough to deal with without concerning himself with the likes of me. As a parent myself, all these years later, all these heartbreaks later, I understand now, at least a little bit. A few moments later he hugged my mother, beside herself and a leaking faucet in the best of times, two forever tortured souls that would find no rest.

My face was cupped in Mrs. O'Malley's soft hands as she pulled me in and kissed my forehead, gazing into my soul. Then she melted into Margaret's arms—collapsed really—exhausted. Yes, I remember that specific moment, the moment the blur of the week came into focus and it all became real. Susan was gone and we were still here—us, we, the collateral damage.

Paddy was standing by his mother's side. He looked up

at me with a boyish curiosity, his hair combed and clean, and leaned in to say something, but decided against it. He had something on his mind, something important to him, but he feared it was unimportant to anyone else, like he wanted to ask if he could show me his new red Schwinn with the white banana seat and baseball cards proudly clothes-pinned to the spokes, but lost his will. I looked down and told him I was sorry, but he didn't react to my words, just stared up at me like he'd met his hero and was disappointed. Perhaps he misunderstood my intent or had gone numb to the day, still in the blur and denial and the shock behind the scenes.

In my warm bed, in the comfort of my parent's home, behind the walls of the house where I grew up, I decided I would never again allow informality or close bonds, deeming them too dangerous and unforgiving. Going forward, my life would be loosely bundled and tied, a burlap sack filled to the brim with apathy and formal correspondence, hung from a mail crane and hooked by a passing train, ever moving, a slave to fundamentals and structure. I would exist on the periphery even though I could be seen in the shadows. There would be Margaret and Thomas, formal and angular, no Maggie and Tom, Susie or Sue. Lillian, of course, would become Lily—we all have our weaknesses.

There's a photo of Susan I took in the student union. She's posed—there was no sneaking a candid of her—seated in one of those seventies bean-bag chairs, oddly plump and fake leather, all puff and plush, armed with a devilish look, half fighting to not have her picture taken at all, the other half modeling, campy and inviting. She'd been sticking her tongue out at me, that tease of hers that made me squirm and I hurried to catch her in the act, languorous and provocative, but, like much in her life, fleeting. I struggle to dig Margaret's camera out of my duffle and I was moments too late, regrettably. Her curled tongue had returned to her mouth, but in the image, in the moment, her personality endures. That is how I want to remember her—the playful vamp in a tight knit sweater always leaving me wanting more, leaving the world wanting more.

An apology is warranted. When I speak of Susan, it's often in that flash of hormonal zeniths and emotions so prominent of the age, the all-or-nothing paradox that influences the fabric of our social existence, our very existence. That's not my intent or, at least, not my singular intent. That blood pumping, raging through our bodies is, of course, what gives the memories their gloss, what makes them more vivid and meaningful even so many years later. But, I would not be painting a complete picture if I failed to mention she was, first and foremost, my best friend. How rare and wonderful a life that is drawn to opposing sides of the magnet. How cherished this life must be. On the top of a hill, near a sentinel, wide-armed oak, with a view of a valley, we buried her. I miss my friend.

Over the past forty years, there are times when I gather the courage to visit Susan's grave. I used to visit often, but now, only sometimes. I talk to her, but she doesn't answer. There are times when I feel her hand on my shoulder and my neck and I get that shiver she always managed to give me. Most times I find a cozy spot under Susan's oak and think about her laugh while I look at her resting place. Of course, her laugh and her face have faded over time to the point where maybe I don't really remember them much. Maybe they're now an amalgam of memory and invention, the lines softened and blended, the best of what I would like to remember about her and about myself and about how we were together.

Sometimes I read a book and almost fall asleep. Or I talk to Susan about Lily and how she's doing in school and her dance recital and the friends she may have for life—like we could have been. Like we were supposed to be. They would have liked each other, Susan and Lily. They have the same mischievous sense of humor and the confident ability to laugh at themselves that I sorely lack. I wonder what Lily would be like if she were the offspring of Susan and myself. But, then she would not be Lily, our Lily, the Lily we have now, and I dismiss the thought. Dreams should not come at the expense of the living.

There was the time when I told Susan about Lily's first boyfriend and, of course, what I thought of him. Lily was maybe eight years old and it was really just a boy at school, someone in her homeroom. When I laughed, I thought I heard Susan laugh. I felt safe sharing these things with her, a comfort in knowing she knew there was a life that carried on, unburdened. At least that was comforting to me. Susan's laugh became more common over time, a soft, thorough laugh that shook her body and made me laugh—at least that's how I want to remember it. Come to think of it, it's possible Susan's laugh, the one I remember, is actually part of Margaret's laugh, merged and intertwined over the years. But, to be honest, Margaret doesn't laugh much anymore and I find it difficult to remember either laugh with any confidence. I know that's my fault and my fault alone.

There was one fall morning, steeped in thick New England fog, where I swear I saw her, Susan, standing near her resting place at the peak of the hill. I was at the bottom of the hill, looking up toward her. I rubbed my eyes and squinted, thinking the fog, and perhaps the morning itself, was playing its tricks. I pulled in a deep breath through my nose, taking in the mid-October air, damp and slightly chilled, almost sweet, while she stood, alive as the day, on the yellowing grass and fallen leaves that littered her own grave. She was dressed in unfamiliar clothing, a hip-length, tan raincoat belted tight at the waist and some sort of greenish rubber mud boots pulled to just below the knee, like someone who planned to be about for a long while. Her head was bowed low, shoulders hunched forward and her hair, darkened by the years and cut into a sort of bob, fell loosely over the side of her face.

My shoes clopped and scraped along the damp asphalt as I unconsciously picked up pace after passing beneath the stone archway that served as the St. Mary's cemetery gate. I wasn't quiet. Yet, she didn't hear me as I climbed the hill, or perhaps ignored me while deep in whatever ethereal plane she occupied. I stopped under my resting tree and stood behind her, lurking in the mist for what felt like ten minutes, observing, studying the lines of her body, her waist, the way her raincoat glowed in the gray of morning, her still as a broken night. I thought there were whispers, faint words of prayer maybe, leaking from her lips, breaking the pressed stillness. Finally, far from composed and beyond hope, I called to her: "Mrs. O'Malley."

Oddly, she didn't jump or appear surprised to see me, or to see someone at least. She turned her head and smiled. "Thomas!" she said like we'd casually run into each other at the grocery first thing on a Sunday morning.

She pulled me in for a deep hug and kissed my cheek. I felt the wet of her cheek, at once both warm and cold and felt the immense guilt of having disturbed her.

"I'm so sorry to disturb you," I said.

"Nonsense," she said then took a moment to find the right words. "It makes me happier than I can say that you still remember Susan, that you come to visit her."

"I think of her every day," I said. And I do.

"Walk me to my car," she said. "I'll let you have your time with her."

We walked together down the hill, her arm wrapped around my waist, mine around hers, her head tight against my collarbone and for more than a brief moment, it was Susan, and we walked together like it would have been.

"How's my Lily?"

"Loud and fast," I chuckled.

"She's going to break hearts, that one."

"Afraid so," I said.

She stopped at the bottom of the hill, near the stone archway and released me. She began to cry again and took my face in her hands, my stubbly, unshaven face rough to the touch. I hoped she could not smell the gin on my breath.

"Will you give my love to Margaret?"

"Yes, of course."

"She's a good one," she said in that approving, motherly tone and I nodded.

Her hands, dry and strong, held me in their grip for several seconds longer, her lips, pinkish white, twitching, attempting to flex and bend, to form a word, to say something, forming the "O" of Susan's funeral. She looked over my shoulder, toward the hill and the oak tree and the grave. She patted my chest with an open palm as she pulled away.

"Goodbye…" she said weakly, her voice trailing off before she melted into the still heavy morning fog, the day only beginning to warm. I wondered for weeks afterward whether I had actually seen Mrs. O'Malley, held her waist while we walked, noted a faint perfume of flowers or merely dreamt it all. It seemed so real, so necessary, but I can't be sure.

On occasion, Margaret accompanies me on that walk up the hill where whatever is left of Susan lies buried six feet down. The weathered gray headstone is sorely in need of a scrubbing and the grass could always afford a mow. Of course, I'm not myself when Margaret is there, not my solemn "cemetery" self anyway. When we visit together, it's more about Margaret and I do my best to be sure of it. It's not that I purposely hide or am embarrassed by grief or emotion. All of it, of course, is natural. It's more that it's Margaret's time and I step aside and let her be with Susan, free to speak or pray or share. It's important to know when a day, a moment, is not yours.

When Susan was gone, darkness took her place at the table. For me, I filled the chair with gin and distance and apathy. For Margaret, she found more positive ways to fill the empty time. At home, Margaret still feeds the animals that congregate on our outside patio—the squirrels and birds and ducks. For so many years I wondered why she continued to feed the furred and feathered, what purpose it provided, this interfering with nature. The regulars were fat with peanuts and seed and slices of cheesecake for all I know, well insulated for any bleak season. It made little sense to me that, regardless of the weather, Margaret was diligent in attending to the insatiable little beggars. I remained confused for many years until I realized this ritual, this small act of kindness, served as her relief from a churning, restless mind, one that spent the minutes, hours, days justifying its very existence and wondering what it offered the world.

20

May is my favorite month of the year. The trees and grass reach their sexual zenith and spew forth clouds of orgasmic pollen. The world is covered in the sneezing and coughing of the yellowish bliss. In May, New England begins to warm, throwing off the shackles and chill of March and April, performing the long, comfortable inhale before the steamy exhale of hot, humid summer. Sandwiched between April's fickle temperature mood swings and June's irrational sun, May compels us to venture forth, to crawl out of our stifling northern burrows, clear our eyes and explore the world. May is hope. May is rebirth. May is also the month I was going to ask Susan to be my wife.

May is also death. Not the death we all secretly hope will come for us in the pitch of night during our ninth decade, the hooded figure pressing his white hands to our throat and slowly, painlessly draining our breath while our soul is transferred, before judgment, to the black burlap satchel draped over a bony shoulder. No, May is not this death, the one where those left behind celebrate a long life well lived, where tears flow for the grace of time they walked in our presence. Not this May. Not this death. Not at twenty years old. Rotting in a box. In the ground.

It was May 22, 1978. The semester had ended a week or so earlier and Mother's Day came and went without fanfare. I arranged to pick up Susan at her parent's house and drive up the coast to Ogunquit, Maine, more specifically, an ocean side path called Marginal Way. Marginal Way is a winding walkway that essentially connects Ogunquit beach with Perkins Cove; the views make it a place popular with tourists and artists alike. Dotted with scrubby pines and thick tumbles of thorn bushes, the pathway twists along the cold, relentless Atlantic as churning blue and green waves break on the rocky coastline in fits of white foam and salt mist. In my mind, it possesses both the serene and violent, along with a tinge of the romantic. And it cast the perfect backdrop to begin a marriage in earnest.

That morning Susan was oddly agitated, eyes darting back and forth, resting on top of deep black circles, like she'd not slept a moment during the night. She never looked directly at me between her sighs and elongated breaths. She slept most of the drive, pushed as far away from me as possible, across the vinyl and fabric bench seat, burrowed against the passenger side window, using her arm as a pillow, flattened against blue veins and translucent skin. She cracked open the window just a sliver, a quarter turn of the handle, pulling in cool morning air while we drove, the wind frantically tossing wisps of her hair like it had not a care in the world. When she wasn't sleeping or trying to sleep, she was searching through her denim pocketbook with the leather tassels, digging and scratching about for something, staring into the distance as she dug deeper and more aggressively, as if not looking directly at it would somehow cause the lost object to reveal itself. I didn't ask what she was searching for, what was lost, and it may be she was simply keeping herself occupied to avoid conversation.

What was most apparent and what I did not want to admit to myself was that she didn't want to be there. There was more than one moment, especially when we slowed to a stop sign or red traffic light that I thought she might pull the door latch, throw open the door and spring from the car in full step, disappearing into some swamp or forest, never looking back.

Something wasn't right.

During the last week of the semester, and the weeks since, she'd grown increasingly indifferent and distant. As I grew more determined to ask her to marry me, she became uncharacteristically aloof. This perceived indifference, in turn, made me more needy and desperate for her attention. It was a troublesome combination. How much of it was real and how much was merely in my head, my own insecurities run amuck? It was impossible to know.

Still, I was determined to ask her to marry me, to smooth over this rough patch. I bought a ring for a few hundred dollars by working in the college library and cutting lawns over the summer. It was nothing special really, the ring, but it was a diamond and shiny and she liked shiny things and she seemed to like me. I never got the chance to give it to her and a few weeks later I returned to Marginal Way and, with every ounce of strength, threw the cursed ring into the Atlantic. Perhaps it remains there, buried beneath forty years of sand and fish piss. Or maybe it caught the attention of some eagle-eyed scuba diver in search of lobsters, a glittery treasure exposed by the sunlight and now on the finger of someone's wife, none the wiser. Either way, I hope it worked out for the better.

A few minutes after turning right off US 1 in Ogunquit, I found parking on a tidy side street in front of a stately white colonial with black shutters and red brick walkway. Susan flung open the door and sighed again, though I couldn't see her, this sigh, this shrill exhale, would have superbly matched an apathetic roll of the eyes. She dragged herself out, slid onto the pavement then closed the car door with the subtle care of raging field artillery. I attempted to brighten her mood by pointing out our luck at finding parking in front of this impressive home. She didn't respond or if she did, it was without much enthusiasm. I fought the impulse to ask her what was wrong, a mistake I'd made on several occasions in the past. If her mood was dark, it would need to brighten on her terms and her timeline. There were no shortcuts, no whimsical words or clever contortions of my face to shave off time. She would work through it herself, find balance for whatever was in need of rebalancing.

This mood though, this tentacle of the beast, was a bit strange to me as her silence and unresponsiveness were not part of the usual rhythm. Normally—it's still scary to suggest her struggle had a normal and this was not it—there were bouts, nasally starts and stops, of uncontrollable and inconsolable tears. This opening of the pressure valve was a slow, whistling release, a lamb, damp and shivering in the night field, hoping the fox would find another, even less fortunate soul. I didn't know what to make of her current state and instead plodded my way forward, my scheme, at least in my head, underway.

It was a drowsy Monday morning and before the start of the high season so the town was empty—we had Marginal Way essentially to ourselves. There were a few retirees squeaking about in their white tennis shoes and socks pulled high to the knee, gray haired and smiling, walking hand in hand, some slowly, others keeping time. The songbirds were returning to southern Maine and our walk was serenaded by their songs of spring. There was a light breeze from the east, more a breath, cool and soft on my cheek.

The ring was tucked into the front pocket of my jeans where it felt overly heavy and important for something so delicate. I kept putting my hand into my pocket, an awkward, obsessive gesture to make sure the ring had not been lost, not fallen through a phantom hole at the bottom of the thin white pocketing fabric. The moment—my moment, *our* moment—was charging forward and, I thought with undue confidence, could not be stopped by man, beast or act of God. My chest tightened in anticipation. I thought I might throw up right there on the pathway, double over at the waist and retch... what? I hadn't been able to eat anything that morning nor the night prior so there was little in my stomach to empty.

Somewhere along the path and while walking hand in hand, she remarked that I was crushing her hand in my grip. She drew it away and gave me a dark, scolding look while she shook the hand back to life. My meaty paws combined with the tension and anxiety of the moment had failed to set the mood to the warm temperature I would have liked. As usual, I was oblivious to how heavily my hand was holding hers, wrapped around her delicate bones like a vice, how I was not to let go, ever. No doubt I provided a dismissive look as she worked the blood back toward her fingers.

"It hurt!" she said, emphasizing a high whine to make sure I understood.

I shrugged like a goon.

A few moments later, Susan's frown still fresh, we passed a couple of other college age kids, two girls confident in tight, white cotton shorts and tighter, barely there knit tops. Why do I remember them? Did I gawk at them as we passed along the narrow pathway, as we politely squeezed to one side to let them pass? It's possible I said "Hi" or one of them said "Hi" and I responded. Did I look back at them as they passed, peer over my shoulder to get a better, no less inno- cent view?

To this slight, real or imagined, Susan grew furious.

"Do you like her?" she asked.

"What?"

"That girl, the cute one with the dark hair. Do you like her?"

I looked back toward the girls as they rounded a corner and faded from sight. "No."

"Sure as hell seemed like it," she continued. "Why don't you go ask her out?"

"What are you talking about?"

"I'm not stopping you."

"I'm not interested in that girl."

"Well, you can't be interested in me."

"Why not?"

"Because you can't be."

"I asked you here because I want to marry you."

"What?"

"I want to marry you." My hand dug into my jean's pocket in search of the ring.

"You can't."

"Why not?"

"Because I'm pregnant."

"What?"

"I'm pregnant."

"Pregnant?"

"Yeah. Still wanna marry me?"

"Yes."

"I don't know if it's yours."

"What?"

I fingered the ring in my pocket, turning it over, sliding it on to the tip of my pinkie finger, a false god, my mind racing, my short life flashing in front of me, my legs turned to jelly. I thought I might throw up yet again. My heart was breaking. I collapsed in the middle of the path, legs crossed in front of me, my mouth hung open like I was trying to catch flies. My eyes grew hot around the edges. Did I even know Susan? For a brief moment I've spent a lifetime regretting, I didn't feel love for her. I didn't feel anything at all.

Without a further word, she left the path and, without hesitation or fear, climbed down the jagged rocks toward a flat shelf of water-honed rock, likely covered by several feet of water during the king tide, extending toward the ocean. Once she reached the flat, she removed her flip-flops, leaving them behind, one right-side-up and one turtled on its back. At the water's edge, she took off her t-shirt, and, to my amazement, removed her bra, dropping both at her feet. Her brownish-red nipples, bared to the spring sun, and a freckled shoulder turned slightly, perhaps out of sudden modesty. She held her hands high to the sun, toward heaven, and stood for a few moments in the growing heat of the day. Then she unbuttoned her jeans and pulled them down, then her panties, leaving them all in a heap piled up to her ankles. There she was, the curve of her bottom, her bared spine a shallow trench running the length of her back, ivory skin set free to the world, her hair, halfway down her back, fiery in the sunlight. This, all of this, was steeped in a calm I never thought possible, a deep breath before a cathartic release of her troubles. And did I see a small bump? A small human set to be hatched, curled and contorted above that compact puff of reddish hair near the pubis? Was it possible or merely a specter of my imagination and terror?

I called to her, "What are you doing?"

She didn't answer and, for a yet another reason I've

spent my life searching to find, I stood back on the path, watching the spectacle unfold with an odd curiosity. Who was this nude woman posed in the distance, hands to the sun: Susan, Sue or Susie?

Free of her clothing, she calmly waded from the rocks into the cold Atlantic, small waves causing her to list back and forth. When she was waist deep, she turned to me and mouthed something, smiled, then swam for a few yards before diving beneath the surface, the water rippled by a footed splash, the white of her back fading, a foot the last I saw of her.

She was too far away for me to either hear or even read her lips. What did she say to me? It haunts me that I still don't know. Was I even meant to know?

Was it:

"Goodbye."

"I love you."

"I hate you."

"I'm sorry."

"Forgive me."

I don't know.

And then.

And then, she didn't resurface. She did not swim back to shore. She did not return to me. There were clothes in a pile sitting on the flat, sundrenched rocks, the squawk of gray gulls, a slight ocean breeze and nothing more. Minutes passed. Susan was gone.

How many times can a heart be broken in one day?

21

Patrick and Tom sit across from each other at the kitchen table, neither speaking, neither knowing who should break the silence. I set down three cups of coffee, milk and several iterations of sweetener, then take my place at the table between them. There's a presence in the room, something unsaid, a filthy shard of glass waiting in the lush green lawn for a fat, shoeless foot to bumble upon it.

We'd attended to Tom and brought him back inside, gave him a glass of water. He seemed recovered from whatever state of confusion he'd conjured up, ready to consider Patrick's real intentions. I suppose I too was curious as to his reasons for the visit. I understood his curiosity and desire to learn more about his sister, but what bubbled below the surface? What compelled him on this journey?

"So," Patrick says and closes his eyes, looking for strength to begin. "There's more to my visit then I've let on."

"I gathered that," I say. Tom looks at me out of the corner of his eyes, his jaw rigid, tense.

Patrick begins again and licks his lips. "Several weeks ago I received a phone call from the American Psychiatry Association and I was asked to meet at their office in Boston. They didn't provide a lot of detail other than that it was about Susan."

This time I provide the sideways glance toward Tom. Tom is busy adding more sugar to his coffee, forty years on and I'm still shorting him on the sweetener, but I'm sure Patrick has his full attention.

"That's an odd phone call to receive after all these years," I say.

Patrick nods. "So, we set a time to meet maybe two weeks later so I spent two weeks running through a thousand scenarios—what could this be about? What I can tell you is that it wasn't something I'd considered, not something I expected.

"When I got there, they were almost being too nice, if you know what I mean, making sure I was comfortable and bringing water and coffee. It was a little unsettling. I was just waiting for the punch line, my hands tucked onto my lap, starting forward, wondering what I'd gotten myself into.

"They told me her doctor at Stevens College, Dr. Inslee, had died a few years earlier."

"He must have been late eighties," I say.

"Something like that, yeah. At some point before he died, he'd given his files, all of them, I guess, to a Miss Kerr."

"No idea," I say. Tom shrugs.

"It turns out she was the nurse in his office for thirty years and he wanted her to be the keeper of his research and patient files. Kind of a curator—maybe to eventually donate to the college for scholarly research."

"Oh, I remember her. Pain in the ass," I say with a snarled lip.

"Over time, Miss Kerr started organizing everything, especially Inslee's notebooks he kept on each patient and on a few of them, all females, she noticed some troubling trends and notations, patterns."

"Their behaviors were similar?" Tom asks.

"Yes, but not his patients. Inslee himself."

Tom looks at me again; his bottom lip twitches. Patrick has our full attention.

"He was administering shock treatment for all of them—girls, young women—and in order to relax them before each treatment, he was giving them narcotics. That, in and of itself, wasn't the issue. That was reasonably standard for the treatment, but what was unusual was they were all being given a dose higher than their weight would suggest.

"She brought it to the attention of a Dr. Marquez at the Psychiatry Association to see if they could provide some clarity. He was the one who called me for the meeting. They figured the doses were likely increased for a specific purpose and reached out to each of the patients affected, the ones they could track down at least."

"Why would he increase the doses?" I ask.

"Rape," Tom mumbles from the edge of the table.

"Exactly," Patrick responds.

"So he raped them when they passed out?"

"Yes. And he booked a lot of appointments over the years."

"And Susan?" I ask.

"She was one of the victims. How often, we'll never know."

"Oh my God," I whisper. "Did she know?"

"I don't know," Patrick says and claps his hands together indicating this is the extent of his knowledge.

"She knew," Tom says and looks at me, then Patrick, elbow on the table and chin tucked into his palm, his eyes sliding across his face. "She told me. I just didn't understand what she meant until now."

Then Tom's face falls calm, almost relaxed, and his mouth hangs open as he leans back. His question, *the* question, it seems, has been answered.

As Patrick is about to pass through the door, perhaps out of our lives forever, it's my turn, my moment to be selfish.

"Patrick, did your parents receive a report from the coroner's office after she died?" I ask, a question forty years in the making.

"They did, yes," he replies. "I have it stored with the rest of her photos and other paperwork."

"I assume then your parents read the report and you read it?"

"I did, yes."

"I hope you don't mind me asking, but did they find any drugs in her system?"

"That was really my parents' first question, right—part of the why and the how."

"Of course."

"They wanted to know if they missed something, some sign, some behavior, clues. You know—was there something else going on with Susan, was there an accelerant, so to speak."

Tom and I continue to nod along, our heads swiveling on pliable neck bones, well stretched by the continued conversation. I wait patiently, trying to hide the intensity of my query. Had Susan taken the hit of acid that day, the hit of acid meant for me?

"So," Patrick continues. "My parents asked for the toxicology report and I can't really say which outcome they hoped to read. Was it better that she was under the influence or that her illness had caught up to her?"

"She was complicated," Tom says, breaking his silence.

"Very," Patrick continues. "As it turns out, there was a little of both."

I shuffle in my shoes, dragging them along the floor in nervous anticipation.

"They found a pill in her pants pocket, but nothing in her system."

"Clean?" I ask.

"Clean," he answers and shrugs. "At least at that moment in time."

I settle back into the chair and begin to cry.

Afterword

I'd forgotten how beautiful Margaret is, inside and out. How blind I've been, how foolish, how awful. I guess understanding and discovering is living, finally. It's better than never having lived. The excuses have run their course, called out for the shams they always were.

As all indulgences must end, so too does my drinking, at least according to that shiny young doctor of mine, the one with the slight build, bony elbows and brown widow's peak, dark brown eyes below bushy eyebrows and a child's sun-freckled skin. He's pleasant enough to look at, though his nose hair needs a trim. There are a few unruly hairs intent on making an escape, flying out of his nostrils in random directions as a lark. I haven't pointed it out to him. Margaret doesn't think I should. I've been drinking longer than he's been alive. I was probably belly to a bar and ten drinks deep the night of his wobbly back seat conception. Oddly, when I point out this little gem, he either doesn't understand or maybe doesn't care. I can't tell which.

Diabetes, I'm told, has taken root, the painful bluish sores on my feet a telltale sign of this old man scourge. The young doctor has informed me they—my feet that is—could soon worsen to the point where they would require a complete lopping off near the knee. Stumps. I joked to Margaret that at least with my natural conveyance disabled, I'd be prevented from running away from my thoughts. Her sense of humor is not what it once was. Or perhaps I was never very funny. As for me, the teaching of tricks to old dogs is unsettling and unappreciated, and I suspect the gin and the diabetes will continue to flow unabated, hand in hand like two drunk lemmings skipping carefree and high-kneed toward the cliff's edge. After all, Lily is an adult and Margaret is an adult and it's within my rights to choose to be a child. There is only action or inaction, and I chose my team long ago.

The doctor with the bony elbows, I can only assume, knows my path forward, the path I'll choose, and looks at me with faint, but certain disappointment, nodding those bushy eyebrows and releasing a weak, "Ok?" to a condemned man. I think in these modern times they have training for such things in medical school, sensitivity to the difficult and stubborn patient, the impossible and lost cause. Whereas in the past I would have been due (and received in short order) a stern talking to, a sit down at the big desk in his office, door closed, the room smelling of hardwood and lousy with diplomas, degrees and certificates, him using a firm tone to rehash the dangers we've already hashed. Now there's a tendency to treat me as a lost cause, to leave me to my own devices, to treat me like I'm an adult. His work is done. I didn't expect him to surrender so easily, but he may be thankful for the time saved so he can work on his putting at the country club.

Well, isn't this just great?

Margaret, of course, will want me to follow some regimen of sea salt and mushrooms she read about in one of her glossy monthlies, something keen on reducing blood sugar. There will be changes, no doubt, to our diets, the addition of evening walks to promote blood flow and the like, more bottles and glasses and gallons of tasteless water pumped and packaged from some fancy-sounding valley or mountain or underground aquifer, complete with a fancy-colored label and a price tag beefier than a quart of motor oil. The poor fool. Does she know me at all? I've been searching for an out for over forty years. Why would I throw away this opportunity—fancily wrapped in reflective and wondrous gold foil paper and adorned with a delicate bow?

Family life is lighter, less encumbered these days, like the barnacles were scraped clean from Lily's skiff. Gary and his over-wrought father, Gary Sr., are now a memory, at least as much as any former spouse and family can be. Like my foot's destiny, they've been lopped off, though rather than with a doctor's hacksaw, by the decree of divorce. Of course, I can empathize with the Garys and maybe, given time, even forgive them for their faults. They're scoundrels after all, more my people than not. It's possible I'll miss them and their meandering tales of fortune, but it doesn't mean I have to care for them. And for the first time in longer than I can remember, Lily has a bounce in her step, a bounce of the unburdened. We all do.

The house is smaller and less lonely. It's turned into a home, perhaps for the first time. Each room has gained warmth and coziness, the air a bit heavier like someone friendly has already breathed it in. There are myriad knick-knacks—glass things collected over the years, pale porcelain dolls sitting in crevices I haven't noticed since Lily was a child. Some objects I'm seeing for the first time: a crucifix passed down by Margaret's grandmother hangs crooked in the living room and a framed picture of our wedding day sits on an end table, the brown wood frame dusted and protective glass wiped clear like it was set down only yesterday. Until I rediscovered the wedding photo, I'd forgotten Margaret's smile.

Even the quiet is less quiet. After all, what is a home devoid of people? Now, there are conversations and toothy grins and time spent together in the same room. I'm not sure what we talk about or if any of it is of particular importance, but it doesn't matter much. Another welcome surprise: dinner tastes better, like we've finally discovered exotic spices in the cabinet, cleverly tucked behind the worn, spotted cow salt and pepper shakers. Against all odds, I'm even enjoying mashed potatoes again. It seems so natural now, this existence in a happy home.

Margaret has asked me to stay. She's asked me to do better, to work on improving my health. She's asked me to live, for her and for Lily. And I will, at least a little longer. And I will tell Margaret that I love her and I will thank her for the past forty years and for tomorrow. I'll kiss her goodnight and good morning. I'll remember to call her Mags, like the old days, when we were young.

⌒

At night when the lights are out and Tom's body is near me, I think he finally sees me, the real me, not a ghost, not a memory, but me, flesh and blood. We begin the end of our lives renewed, like our vows have returned home after a years-long wandering.

Gone is young Tom, the svelte college freshman with thick curly hair, straight shoulders and a pale, pimpled complexion. He's been replaced with a slightly—perhaps not so slightly—rounder version, thicker around the middle and slower to rise from the sofa. Old Tom—he doesn't appreciate that moniker, who would?—has more hair than young Tom though not in the traditional places. The hair has moved south, perhaps toward a warmer climate, leaving the north exposed to the elements and above the tree line. In between the thinning hair of his scalp, there are small brown sunspots and new gray sprouts that dare to pierce the surface only to whither in the drought of late middle age. The pimples on his face have been replaced with whiskers, thick brown rascals mixed with gray, unruly on occasion, filthy most of the time. At least we're aging together.

A few times a year, I take a drive toward the coast, the long way, down Massachusetts Route 133, winding through North Andover and Boxford, to Stevens College.

The moment I see those iron gates—the archway curled and twisted into black metal vines—I'm eighteen again, rosy cheeks and tight ass stuffed into faded blue jeans, long hair threatening the small of my back. All it takes is that first view of campus to transport me—I'm home again. The trees (oaks and red maples) were often leafless during the semester, yet when I see them on a summer day, they're both perfect and just right, matching my romanticized recollections real and imagined. In the days before the weight of the real world, we laughed, we drank, we inexplicably avoided arrest. After all these years, the memories come roaring back like they were yesterday—did we really run naked through the quad on a dare and Southern Comfort?—and I can't help wondering how we managed to survive some of the nonsense. Not all of us did. I suppose none of us did.

On the second floor of William Lewis Library, tucked into a dusty corner, there's a plaque in memorandum with Susan's picture, her beauty frozen in time, her troubles invisible save a strict accounting of her days: February 3, 1958— May 22, 1978. You could spend a week in the library, exploring every floor and aisle, each nook and closet, and not take notice of her. I stop and visit her often. She's more alive here than the cemetery—now that sounds silly—her memory is more relatable in this corner, artificially warmed in the winter, cooled in the summer, comfortable. It's much more a beginning than the gravestone's end, or at least it's the middle. The cemetery, of course, is a bit more peaceful than the library's hustle and bustle, but Susan was never at peace, often in a good way.

Tom even walked campus with me last week, the first time we'd been on campus together in a long time. We visited Susan's picture and afterward Tom was lighter than usual, and did I even catch a smile sneaking through those whiskers? I asked what made him smile and he said it was a long time since he remembered Susan, not what happened to Susan.

⌒

"Mom," Lily said recently. "I've never seen you so happy." Then she followed with: "You look really good— wait, you're not having an affair are you?"

"Yes," I told her. "I am. With my husband."

One Sunday, I took Lily and Tom to the ice cream shop on Route 133, the squat, white cottage barely changed after all these years. We stood in line like dopes, shuffling forward three feet at a time, hands stuffed in our pockets, awaiting some kind of rare and special treat. And it was a special treat—while waiting in line I told them about my father and his passion for ice cream and the laws of nature we defied one day when I was anxious to get back to school. And I told her about the old gas station, long demolished and replaced with a yellow colonial and paved driveway, and about the man who stood there waiting to wash your windshield like it was the most important act of his day. Perhaps it was and in that simpler time it was just what we needed.

Lily wanted to attend Stevens and was admitted, but in the end, I talked her out of it. It was less a talking out and more a refocus on other opportunities, that's how I justi-fied it. How self-serving and irresponsible of me to deny her because of my scars. If Tom had pushed it, had wanted her to go, I would have relented, but there was something he too carried with him—a fear of the past repeating that bought his silence. Maybe the experience of having Lily wander the piss yellow halls and run naked through the quad, as silly as it sounds, would have helped all of us. Maybe a new story, a happier story would've emerged with Lily leading the charge. At least then we would've all been able to share Stevens in a new way. We've managed to let go of much of the past, to place salve on the itching scars, but there is still work to be done.

When Patrick left, after the hugs and thanks and tears, things changed, especially between Tom and me. There will never be complete closure, nor do we want to forget, but this is finally a time where we can move forward, full for-ward. I wish Patrick's visit had come sooner for Lily, because life would've been different—Tom and I less distant and undoubtedly, less ornery. But it's better that it happened at some point so we could ride off into our sunset, our retire-ment not from our careers, but from ourselves. We have the opportunity, Tom and I, to start fresh, to begin near the end and enjoy what's left of our days. It's our look forward, though Susan, our love, will always be in our hearts, watch-ing over us.

www.ingramcontent.com/pod-product-compliance
Lightning Source LLC
Chambersburg PA
CBHW020024310726
48970CB00007B/2191